Impersonations

ALSO BY WALTER JON WILLIAMS

PRIVATEERS AND GENTLEMEN SERIES
(AS JON WILLIAMS)
To Glory Arise (originally *The Privateer*)
The Tern Schooner (originally *The Yankee*)
Brig of War (originally *The Raider*)
The Macedonian
Cat Island

HARDWIRED SERIES
Hardwired
Solip:System
Voice of the Whirlwind

DRAKE MAIJSTRAL SERIES
The Crown Jewels
House of Shards
Rock of Ages

METROPOLITAN SERIES
Metropolitan
City on Fire

DREAD EMPIRE'S FALL SERIES

The Praxis

The Sundering

Conventions of War

Investments

DAGMAR SHAW SERIES

This Is Not a Game

Deep State

The Fourth Wall

SHORT FICTION COLLECTIONS

Facets

Frankensteins and Foreign Devils

The Green Leopard Plague and Other Stories

Ambassador of Progress

Knight Moves

Angel Station

Elegy for Angels and Dogs

Days of Atonement

Aristoi

The Rift

The New Jedi Order: Destiny's Way

Implied Spaces

IMPERSONATIONS

WALTER JON WILLIAMS

A TOM DOHERTY ASSOCIATES BOOK

NEW YORK

IMPERSONATIONS

Copyright © 2016 by Walter Jon Williams

Cover art by Jaime Jones
Cover design by Christine Foltzer

Edited by Jonathan Strahan

A Tor.com Book
Published by Tom Doherty Associates
175 Fifth Avenue
New York, NY 10010

www.tor.com

Tor® is a registered trademark of Macmillan Publishing Group, LLC.

ISBN 978-0-7653-8780-6 (ebook)
ISBN 978-0-7653-8781-3 (trade paperback)

First Edition: October 2016

Introduction

THOUSANDS OF YEARS AGO, Earth and its inhabitants were conquered by the alien Shaa. Along with other alien species within the Shaa imperium, humanity has been subjected to the unforgiving rule of the Praxis, the empire-wide law imposed by the conquerors. Intended to create an ideal, ordered society based on universal and rational principles, the Praxis is enforced by a reign of terror and blood.

Foremost in upholding the Praxis is the order of Peers, the ennobled descendants of the collaborators who helped the Shaa establish their rule. But now, with the last of the Shaa having passed from the scene, the Peers must actually try to run the empire.

The first crack in the Praxis occurred during the Naxid War, when the most senior of the conquered species tried to seize the empire and replace the Shaa with themselves. The Naxids were defeated, in part through the actions of Captain the Lady Sula, but now Sula finds the rewards for her service are exile, on a distant planet called Earth. . . .

THE WOMAN CALLED CAROLINE SULA looked up from her desk to see a mammoth ship poised in the floodlights of the ring. It hovered above the rotating ring like a skyscraper floating free of gravity, its landing lights glaring, nose studded with grapples, probes, and docking tubes all deployed to catch a berth as Earth's antimatter ring rotated beneath it.

Sula's heart gave a lurch at the unexpected sight, and then the ship vanished beneath the floor as the ring continued its rotation. She spun her chair to look behind her, and the big ship reappeared downspin from her office. Maneuvering jets flared against the ship's matte-black flanks, and the ship floated with slow majesty to a gentle berth in the Fleet dockyards.

"What the hell is *that*?" she demanded.

Lieutenant-Captain Lord Koz Parku, who was in the middle of delivering a report on satellite maintenance, raised his gray, expressionless head. "Lady Sula?"

"That ship that just docked. What was it?"

Parku's dark eyes focused over Sula's shoulder at the ship lit by the dockyard's floodlights, a tall irregular tower suddenly sprouting from the ring. "I don't know, my lady."

Sula rose from her desk and walked to the shelf where she kept her binoculars. She put them to her eyes and toggled the on switch.

"It looks like a Bombardment-class heavy cruiser," she said. "But it's got civilian markings. Though what's it doing in the Fleet dockyard if it's a civilian?"

"Shall I find out, my lady?"

"Yes."

Sula frowned. There were no warships in the Sol system that she knew of—her command consisted entirely of transports, vehicles for satellite and ring maintenance, and a swank little cutter for her own personal use. Whatever was going on with the ship, it was irregular, and she was wary of irregularities within her command.

Parku raised an arm and busied himself with his sleeve display. Sula continued to study the ship—the *cruiser*. No one had told her there would be civilian ships in the Fleet dockyard, let alone civilian ships that seemed to have been built to military specifications. And Parku didn't know the answers to her questions because he hadn't been here any longer than she had.

"The ship is the *Manado,* my lady." Parku moved to stand by her as she looked out the transparent wall. His Daimong voice was measured and melodious, though he brought with him the scent of his rotting flesh, not entirely concealed by baths and use of scent. Sula, sensitive to odors, repressed a twitch of her upper lip.

"It was laid down in the shipyards here during the war, as the new *Bombardment of Utgu*. But the war ended before completion, and a civilian company bought it, completed construction, and now operates it."

"Operates it as *what*?" Sula asked.

Parku uttered a brief, chiming tone intended as a placeholder, where a human might insert a "Well ..." or an "Umm."

"'General cargo,'" Parku said finally. "Apparently." His timbre indicated a lack of satisfaction with the answer.

None of this, Sula reflected, made sense. The Fleet was being expanded, both to replace war losses and to build a much larger force less prone to subversion. Even if the war was over, *Bombardment of Utgu* should have been added to the active list.

Irregularities of this sort, Sula thought, generally meant corruption somewhere. Someone had given a ship to an ally in return for a token payment.

But, she reflected, it wasn't *her* corruption; it wasn't her fault or her responsibility. It may not even have been arranged here but in the capital of Zanshaa or somewhere else. It had all happened before she had arrived, three weeks before.

"So, what's *Manado* doing in my dockyard?" Sula asked. "Why isn't it in a civilian berth?"

Again that chiming tone while Parku flicked through his sleeve display. "The Manado Company contracted to rent a berth in the Fleet dockyard." He looked up, his large eyes liquid in his expressionless face. "The contract expires in two months, my lady."

"Do they resupply from the Fleet? Air, antihydrogen? Rations?"

Parku returned to his display. "Yes. But they pay for anything they take from us."

"Generously, I hope."

Parku's timbre conveyed ambivalence. "Their payments would seem to be in line with our costs."

Paranoia stoked Sula's thoughts. "They don't take on *weapons*, do they? Or antiproton ammunition?"

"No, my lady."

Sula frowned at the ship and moved back behind her desk, where the scent of Parku's decay couldn't reach her.

"Find out what you can about the Manado Company," she said. "When you have a moment."

"Yes, my lady."

"And now—you were saying about satellite maintenance?"

Parku finished his report just as the ring rotated out of Earth's shadow and into sunlight. The Fleet had generously given the station commander an office in a small tower overlooking the dockyards, and now blazing Sol etched every detail of the ring and the docked ships with brilliant fire. Parku raised a hand to shade his eyes. Sula raised the sun shield in the eastern quadrant of the office.

"Thank you, my lady," Parku said.

"Is that all, then? You can return to your office."

"My lady." Parku braced to attention, his chin raised, his throat bared in order to expose himself to his superior's lethal punishment. When the punishment did not arrive, he made a smart military turn and left the office.

Sula rotated her chair and contemplated the matte-black bulk of *Manado,* a darkness against the greater darkness of space, and then she shrugged.

Something underhanded had gone on where the ship was concerned, and eventually she might get to the bottom of it.

But not today. In a few hours, she'd begin her vacation.

———

"You won't need parade dress, will you?"

"I hope not," said Sula. "I don't want to have to wear those heavy boots, let alone that leather shako."

She viewed the tall stovepipe headgear that Spence held for her inspection.

"Let's not pack it," she decided.

Spence nodded with relief. "Very good, my lady."

An officer with the rank of captain was expected to travel with an amazing amount of gear—a full set of uniforms for all climates and seasons, equipment for any sports or hobbies she might enjoy, plus of course a complete set of place settings for the dinners she was obliged to host: plates, bowls, cups, and utensils suitable for all the species living under the Praxis, each ideally marked with her family crest or the name of her command. Plus wine and other liquors, delicacies like candied taswa fruit or cashment soaked in vermouth.

Sula's last ship had been outfitted in haste and she hadn't the time to commission all that porcelain, and though she'd hosted dinners for her officers and for her captains, they'd eaten off plain dinnerware from the galley. In fact, she still hadn't acquired the appropriate porcelain, because she'd planned to buy it on Earth, where porcelain had been *invented*. And because she didn't drink alcohol, she was at a loss where wine was concerned; and though she'd served it to others, she had to trust the brokers as to its quality.

Of course, she had dined with her officers on the ring station, but again off plainware from the galley; and if they had any doubts about the wine, they'd kept it to themselves.

"My lady?" Gavin Macnamara appeared in the doorway. "Are we taking sidearms?"

"*You* are," Sula said. Macnamara was a Constable First Class and might, she supposed, be called upon to restore order somewhere. "For myself, I don't plan on shooting anybody." She turned to Spence. "And you?"

Spence looked doubtful. "Is it dangerous down there?"

Macnamara—tall, lean, with a halo of curly brown hair—and Engineer/1st Spence—pug-nosed, sturdy, short, and straw-haired—were the other two survivors of Action Group Blanche, a stay-behind group on Zanshaa intended to lead the resistance against occupying Naxids.

All the other members of the group had been captured and tortured to death. Only Sula's paranoia had managed to keep her own unit alive—paranoia along with a talent for criminality.

Spence and Macnamara were two of the four servants Fleet regulations permitted to captains like Sula. The third was a Cree chef named Turney, for all those banquets, and the fourth slot was currently unoccupied.

"I don't know that Earth is any more or less dangerous than Zanshaa," Sula said.

"That doesn't help," Spence pointed out. She turned to Macnamara and sighed. "I'll take a sidearm. I don't suppose I'll ever wear it."

"Very good." Leaving a faint scent of gun oil, Macnamara returned to his packing.

Other last-minute packing decisions took an hour, and then Sula took a shower and went to bed with her hand comm and a collection of mathematical puzzles. Neither held her attention. Instead, she considered the matter of firearms and how they reflected what sort of person she now was.

The war had been fundamental in shaping her self—she remembered five enemy ships torn to golden plasma streamers at Magaria, and her cry, "*It was Sula who did this! Remember my name!*" For over two years, she'd been a weapon, as purposeful as Macnamara's sidearm, and she'd been very good at being what she was, a nearly feral creature whose sole purpose had been the destruction of the Naxid enemy.

But now the war was over, and Sula had been given a pointless job in a dusty corner of the empire. She was still a weapon, but nobody needed weapons now. She was like *Bombardment of Utgu,* the heavy cruiser renamed *Manado* and set to a peaceful job in a peaceful world.

At least *Manado*'s tasks were necessary for *somebody.* Sula wasn't sure her own job had a point at all: nothing done at the Fleet dockyard had any genuine military purpose; it could all be done by civilian contractors.

But then, there wasn't genuine military purpose any

longer, not anywhere. It was peacetime now.

Sula wasn't allowed to be a weapon any longer. So, what was she now?

Because Sula possessed a certain pride, she did her new job well. She'd spent the first three weeks diving into the workings of the dockyard, bringing personnel up to the mark, making sure the equipment and supplies she'd signed for actually existed, and handing out demerits with a liberal hand. The dockyard was now running well enough that Sula could go to Earth itself and view what her distant ancestors had managed to create in the way of civilization.

But despite all that, Sula wasn't her new job, or vice versa. What was she?

She didn't have an answer.

She looked at the hand comm and checked her messages. There were a few minor issues from the dockyard, easily dealt with. And then she saw another message, *I'm coming to Terra!*, sent by one Lady Ermina Vaswani.

Sula couldn't imagine why she'd care whether someone named Ermina Vaswani was coming to Terra or not, and with a degree of skepticism, she triggered the message.

A woman in her midtwenties appeared on the screen, blond and green-eyed, with a large, noble nose prominent in the center of her face.

"Hi!" she said, in a bright, enthusiastic voice. "It's your cousin Goojie, your best friend from school!"

Sula paused the recording, freezing Cousin Goojie's ardent face.

"Shit," she said.

She called up her own image on the screen and laid them side by side. She and Cousin Goojie shared the same pale blond hair and green eyes. Sula didn't have Goojie's distinctive nose, and Goojie lacked Sula's pale, porcelain complexion. To an objective observer, it wasn't completely implausible they might somehow be related.

Sula rubbed the thick pad of scar tissue on her right thumb, then triggered the message again.

"I'm a Vaswani now, of course," said Goojie. "We have the Toi-ans as patrons, and they have a company with a branch on Terra, so I'm coming out to manage it! I know you're a big hero now, but if you're not too busy being heroic, I hope we can meet and catch up on old times!"

She cocked her head. "Are you still Caro, now that you're all so grand and important? I'm still Goojie, of course, at least to old friends."

All of which, Sula thought, made a certain amount of sense. The Sulas had been an ancient family, rich and influential, with scores of clients throughout the empire. But the previous Lord and Lady Sula had been caught in some kind of complex fraud, and they'd been skinned alive and executed. The money and property had been confiscated. The Sulas had been dispersed and disgraced—Goojie's parents taking a new name like "Vaswani" would have been camouflage—and all the clients would have been reassigned from the Sula clan to new patrons, like the Lai-own Toi-an family.

At the end of all that, Clan Sula had been reduced to a single member, the sole daughter of Lord and Lady Sula.

Caro Sula. Cousin Goojie's old school chum. Who had been shuffled off to the care of distant relatives on the world of Spannan, far from Zanshaa and the capital.

"I hope we'll get a chance to catch up," Goojie went on. "My ship *Benin* is decelerating now and we're scheduled to dock on the ring in less than a month." She raised a hand and gave a little wave. "Bye! For now!"

Sula gestured at the screen and froze Goojie in midwave. Her brain churned. *Best friend in school.*

Best friend in school. *Which* school? Better find out.

"Are you still Caro?"

Well, no. She had never *been* Caro. Caro Sula was dead.

After her parents' execution, Caro had been shipped to Spannan . . . and then bad things just kept happening. Alcohol. Drugs. Unwise relationships.

And in the worst, most unwise decision of all, Caro had become friends with a girl named Gredel. Who was the girlfriend of a gangster, and who bore a striking resemblance to Caro herself, Gredel who had the silver-gilt hair and the emerald eyes and the pale complexion, and who had a talent for mimicry and voices and accents, and who had a miserable life of her own that she was desperate to escape.

Her hand trembled as she looked at the hand comm, at Goojie's frozen face. She remembered the little smile on Caro's face as Gredel pressed the med injector to her neck, the hiss of the drug as it sent Caro into the twilight that had become her home in her empty, sad life. Remembered the flash of Caro's pale hair as it disappeared beneath the dark waters of the Iola River.

Remembered walking up the hill from the river, to Caro's apartment, to take possession of her identity, to become the woman called Caroline Sula.

She was so young then, Sula thought. Seventeen imperial years, fifteen years by the standards of Earth. So fearless.

Sula's bravery had won her fame and decorations in the war, but she'd never dare try anything like that now.

Sula shuddered, closed her eyes, then opened them again because all she saw were the dead eyes of Caro Sula looking at her.

When she'd been on Zanshaa, she'd encountered any number of people who remembered the young Caro

Sula. But they were mostly of an older generation, friends of the late Lord and Lady Sula, and they remembered her as a child, no older than eleven or twelve. What they now encountered had been a young woman, an officer in the Fleet, and soon after that a decorated hero. She'd been able to bluff them.

But could she bluff Caro's best friend from school? A person who knew her intimately?

There was little option but to try.

"It's wonderful to hear from you," she sent Goojie in reply. "I don't remember those days very well—but I re-member *you,* of course. I'm looking forward to seeing you, but I'll be on the planet surface for a long tour start-ing tomorrow. I hope that doesn't complicate things."

I hope you hit your head on a hatch, she thought.

At least she'd have some time for research. Once upon a time, she'd learned everything there was to know about Caro and obsessively memorized her biography. But in the years since, no one had ever challenged her, and even those who'd known Caro accepted her story, and some of the facts had got a little blurred. Clearly, she needed a refresher.

Fortunately, Lady Ermina Vaswani was a Peer, and Peers were very well documented indeed. Genealogies were readily available, and all manner of biographies and monographs existed, many commissioned by Peers or

Peer clans to explain to other Peers how wonderful they were.

Research. Something that Sula was good at.

Sula realized she wouldn't be able to sleep for hours yet, not with the jolt of adrenaline that Goojie's appearance had brought, so before beginning her researches, she went to the kitchen and made herself a cup of tea. She was adding a thick dollop of golden cane syrup when Macnamara entered, wearing official viridian Fleet sleepwear and a nacré velvet dressing gown that Sula had given him as a present, knowing something so grand would make him uncomfortable but wanting him to have it anyway.

"My lady," he said. "You should have called. I would have brought you tea."

"I'm perfectly capable of making tea," Sula said.

She really didn't *need* servants. She was happier keeping her own place tidy, polishing her own shoes, brushing her own tunics, tossing her own salads. She was perfectly self-sufficient in that regard, and she didn't like other people touching her things. But Spence and Macnamara were too precious to dismiss from her life, and so she had to put up with their insistence on making her life easier.

The nacré dressing gown shimmered closer. "Do you need anything else, my lady?"

Sula stirred the tea, put the spoon in the saucer. "No, that's all. I'm sorry if I woke you."

"I wasn't asleep."

"Good night, then."

"Good night, Lady Sula."

Macnamara remained in the kitchen, ever on duty, as Sula carried the tea to her quarters.

What am I going to do with him? Sula thought. *Him and his gun.*

She put her tea down on the bedside table and reached for her hand comm.

First things first. She needed to find out all she could about Caro Sula's best friend.

———

Once upon a time, when she was Gredel, she'd been known as "Earthgirl." She had been obsessed by Terran history, the intricate, complex narrative of ancient humanity before Earth's conquest by the Shaa. Her friends had found her hobby amusing and singularly useless—even humans couldn't work up much interest in the backwater world on which their distant barbarian ancestors had built their rude civilization. And even she, trapped in poverty on the world of Spannan, hadn't ever seen Earth, or could reasonably hope to do so.

She had learned to imitate an Earth accent, a hick dialect even she had found hilarious. Once she'd actually arrived on Earth's ring and taken command of the shipyard, she'd encountered workers born on Earth, and discovered that there were a great many different Earth accents, of which imperial popular culture had absorbed only the most uncouth.

She felt indignation on behalf of humanity when she realized this. Imperial culture had trivialized her species' home world. And then, because she was never far from paranoia, she wondered if this had been done deliberately, to degrade all culture but that imposed by the Shaa conquerors.

But no. To the rulers of the empire and the sophisticated denizens of the capital, all that mattered was the culture of Zanshaa High City, compared to which all else was provincial. Next to Zanshaa, every world was a backwater, and worthy of mockery whether it had once belonged to a single species or not.

Sula had been given the Earth assignment as punishment, by a superior offended by her unorthodox behavior. But Sula was unorthodox enough to rejoice in the assignment and the possibility that she might view all the places and monuments that had filled her imagination when she was young.

SaSuu. Byzantium. Xi'an. The Grand Canyon, the Arch of Macedoin, the pyramids. All wondrous places that had stirred her, that had become her passion as she'd coped with a childhood of poverty, deprivation, and violence.

And now, as she stood in the waiting room before boarding the elevator that would take her to the planet's surface, she looked at the video monitor that showed a view of the blue-and-white world, and thought, *Soon.*

Who was she now? A tourist, she hoped. A happy tourist.

Sula got only a few hours' sleep, the rest spent in a thorough search of available records for Lady Ermina Vaswani. Caro's friend Goojie had been born a Sula, sure enough, but after the fall of the Sulas, her parents had changed their name to that of another relative, a Vaswani, a Peer family largely unknown on Zanshaa but powerful on their provincial home world of Chijimo. To trade the Sulas for the Vaswanis was to drop several levels in the Peer hierarchy.

Nevertheless, Goojie had continued her education on Zanshaa, gone to Remba College for a degree in Praxis theory, and then had celebrated with a tour of vacation spots throughout the empire. Obviously, the Vaswanis had survived with more money than had the Sulas. Goojie had been on Preowyn when the Naxid rebellion broke out, and spent the war there in apparent comfort. Now she was the new Executive Director of the Terran Division of the Kan-fra Company, controlled by her patron

Toi-an clan. Apparently, Kan-fra rented medical equipment to hospitals, clinics, and nursing homes.

It seemed a company safe enough for a new, young Executive Director. Goojie's inexperience and her degree in Praxis theory probably couldn't do much harm.

Probably they couldn't do Sula any harm, either.

Sula turned at the sound of footsteps and saw her own chief of security, Lieutenant-Captain Lady Tari Koridun, as she carefully came down the ramp into the departure lounge. Koridun moved a little uncertainly in one-third normal gravity. The lower part of the ring—"lower" only from the perspective of someone on the planet, not on the ring itself—rotated at the same speed as the planet to which it was tethered, and provided only one-third gee. The "upper" ring, where most people lived and worked, rotated at a greater speed to provide normal gravity.

Koridun bounced a bit on the landing, then braced in salute with her throat bared. She was a Torminel, with thick gray fur striped with rich sable, and to keep from overheating wore only a uniform vest and shorts over her pelt. Her eyes were a deep, distinctive cobalt blue, unusual in her species.

"Koridun?" Sula said. "There's a problem?"

"Nothing to concern you, Lady Commandant." Koridun lisped the words around her fangs. "I've got to go to the planet surface to bring up a prisoner."

Sula was surprised. "Don't you have constables for that?"

"There seems to be some dispute concerning whether the authorities have the *right* prisoner. Since I know Laimak by sight, I decided to go down to Palermo and see to the matter myself."

"Laimak," Sula repeated. She tried to remember where Palermo might be. "That would be the rigger that's overstayed his leave?"

"Yes, my lady."

Laimak was a Torminel name, and the Torminel had no physical characteristics that would confirm ID, such as a human's retina patterns or fingerprint. Eyewitness identification was the most common way to clear up any disputed identity.

Sula rubbed the heavy layer of scar tissue on the pad of her right thumb.

"Can't you do a gene test?" she said.

"There is a dispute concerning who is to *pay* for any such test, my lady. The Palermo authorities have been . . . intransigent."

Sula gave up. Perhaps Koridun's story was true, or perhaps she was using Laimak as an excuse for a bit of leave on Earth. As security in the dockyard consisted almost entirely of breaking up fights, tossing inebriates in the drunk tank, and keeping thieves out of Fleet stores, there was no urgent business to keep Koridun on the ring. She might as well have fun in Palermo, wherever that was.

"Well," Sula said. "It will be a pleasure to share the journey with you."

"Thank you, my lady."

Sula turned to Macnamara and Spence and introduced them to Koridun. They braced in salute.

"Very good," Koridun said, as if she for some reason approved their names. "Bordi, my attendant, is dealing with the baggage."

There was a chime and then a soft-voiced announcement that the elevator car was ready. Sula turned as the double row of airlock doors opened, and then led the others into the car named *Kirinyaga*.

Two stewards in gold-striped uniforms of pale blue offered to assist her entry, but she was reasonably competent in low gravity, declined their offer, and entered the compartment reserved for Fleet officers. There were a glass wall that would gaze out over the planet once the car left its docking bay, video monitors with a selection of entertainments, a small kitchen, a full bar with ornamental brasses sculpted with Earth's wonders, a deep soft carpet both on the floor and ceiling, and luxurious leather-clad acceleration couches suitable for all the species living under the Peace of the Praxis. The recycled air carried a slight taste of cardamom.

Koridun followed into the section, then turned back to Spence and Macnamara with a faint air of surprise.

"You'll find the servants' compartment two or three sections below," she said.

"They can stay," said Sula, a bit more firmly than she'd intended. Koridun turned to Sula and retained her look of mild bewilderment.

Sula was unwilling to explain herself. As far as she was concerned, Spence and Macnamara had earned the right to sit in the company of anyone they wanted. She'd throw Koridun out the door before either of her servants.

But it probably wouldn't do for Koridun to think that.

"Please join me, Lieutenant-Captain," Sula said. "Shall we have refreshments?"

Terrans and Torminel shared similar construction, though Torminel tended to have a stockier physique and a more substantial bottom. They could use the same furniture. Sula and Koridun sat on adjoining couches, and the blue-jacketed stewards brought them menus. Sula ordered tea and pastry, and Koridun a tartare and a hot drink that probably involved blood.

Koridun was being tactful in the presence of a member of another species. Torminel were carnivores, and most of their meals tended to involve recipes a bit messier than tartare.

Sula looked over her shoulder and saw that the stewards had every intention of ignoring Spence and Macnamara. She gave the nearest steward a glare, and with a show of reluctance, he picked up a pair of menus and handed them to the enlisted.

Sula poured a long tawny rope of honey into her tea, sipped, then settled into her couch. The scent of fine leather rose from the cushions.

"I wonder, Lieutenant-Captain," she said, "if you know anything about the *Manado* that I saw in the dockyard yesterday."

"I know they rent space in our dockyard," Koridun said. "Otherwise, the Manado Company is very secretive."

"Do you know what they're trying to do?"

Koridun lapped at her drink, licked a drop of scarlet from her lower lip. "I can guess, my lady. I think they're exploring the outer reaches of the system. Looking for a planetoid or some other resource they might exploit."

Sula considered this. Koridun's speculation seemed reasonable.

"Do you have any hard evidence?"

"No. But *Manado* is gone for months at a time. They bring back very little, just some cases that might be samples or instruments, and that we aren't allowed to look at."

"Do they carry shuttles? It would be difficult to land something as big as *Manado* on a planetoid, and much easier to use a shuttle. If it's samples they're after, I mean."

"I saw two shuttles strapped onto the ship."

Sula nodded, sipped again at her sweetened tea. "Another speculation, then, if I may. Why the Fleet dockyard and not one of the civilian docks?"

Koridun tapped her fork lightly against the side of her plate as she contemplated the question. "I can only guess, but they may intend to reduce speculation about their mission. If they used a civilian dockyard, they'd be operating in full view of their competitors, and there would be a lot of talk. And, frankly, our security is better than that at the civilian docks, which tends to be, ah, *porous*."

"Thank you. You've helped a great deal."

"Pleased to be of service, my lady." Koridun took another swig of her prokaryotic beverage.

There was a chime, and a sonorous Daimong voice informed the passengers that the car was about to depart, and that all travelers should by now be strapped into their couches. The stewards stepped forward to assist, but Sula and the others managed to buckle themselves in without help.

There was another, more urgent chime, and the same voice said that the car would be under one point seven gravities for the first few minutes of the descent. Sula took a gulp of her tea and placed the cup and saucer on the telescoping table provided for the purpose.

A third chime, and then acceleration pushed Sula into her couch. *Kirinyaga* shot free of its tunnel, and suddenly Earth was visible through the glass wall, a great blue-white plate poised above Sula's head, its outlines hazed with atmosphere. The brilliant cloud formations were as big as continents.

The elevator car crackled and shivered under acceleration.

"Have you been to Terra before, my lady?" Koridun asked.

"No. But I've studied the history here."

"I'm afraid I know very little."

Sula smiled. "It's a specialized subject."

Kirinyaga's acceleration continued. Even before it launched, the car was theoretically at escape velocity—any ship released from dock on the ring would be thrown free of Earth even if it never lit its engines—and so the car had to overcome its own outward potential energy before it could begin its plunge toward the planet. But soon, *Kirinyaga* was well on its way and acceleration eased to one Earth gravity. The recorded Daimong voice told passengers that they could unstrap from their couches and walk freely in their assigned area.

Sula spent the hours strolling, in desultory conversation with Koridun and in drinking sweetened tea. For the most part, though, she just watched as Earth grew larger. She could make out the beige-and-green landmasses, the profound blue of the deep ocean, the silver serpents of rivers writhing through green landscapes. Lightning coiled over storm clouds, flashed like a semaphore transmitting in an unknown language. And slowly the great line of darkness advanced over the Pacific as night's terminator swept along on its eternal mission, leaving behind islands of light and the uneasy flashes of storms.

She had seen all this on other worlds—on Zanshaa itself—but somehow, this was special. Earth had long been the planet of her dreams, and she possessed the notion that she would feel at home there, comfortable in a way that she hadn't felt at Zanshaa, in the Cheng Ho Academy, or even living on her own home world of Spannan.

Earth was ancient. Earth's primeval stones would murmur in her ear, speak to her daughter in a voice both consoling and filled with the melancholy, hard-earned, disenchanted wisdom of the very old.

Perhaps Earth would even forgive. Who could say?

Because she was senior officer, Sula was able to call for

a soundtrack to her thoughts, and so *Kirinyaga* vibrated to the sound of a massed Daimong chorus, the booming voices a perfect accompaniment to the magnificence of the view.

Everyone strapped in again for the turnover point, where acceleration ceased and the passengers experienced weightlessness. The couches rotated to face what had been the ceiling, and so, in a neat trick of engineering that was a pleasure to watch, did the bar and the kitchen, which were equipped with appliances that could either be flipped or used with gravity going either way. Then deceleration began, gravity built, and the couches settled into their new configuration, along with the rest of observed reality. The carpeted ceiling had become the carpeted floor, and Earth was no longer over Sula's head but below her feet. As soon as she was permitted, she unstrapped and walked to the glass window to give herself a better view.

She had to strap in again for the entry into Earth's atmosphere. Gees built, and *Kirinyaga* rattled on its cable as sheets of flaming ions cascaded past the glass wall and strobed everything in the room with stark, brilliant light.

Eventually, the ride calmed down, and Sula looked up at a dark blue sky, with the thin silver arc of the antimatter ring shining from horizon to horizon. Minor shifts in deceleration tugged at her inner ear. High winds buffeted the car.

A moment of sudden grayness, and then they were through cloud. Sula felt her heart lift.

The Daimong chorus struck a climactic chord as snowcapped Mount Kenya rose silently into view, its pinnacles glowing in the westering sun, its fissures and valleys a deep black. *Kirinyaga* bobbed on its cable, lurched like a terrestrial elevator trying to locate the proper floor, and then the beige buildings of the launch complex rose around them, and the elevator car silently entered its home as the Daimong choir sang out their triumph.

Sula tipped the stewards on her way out, wished Koridun luck in locating her fugitive, and sent her toward the train station and, ultimately, Palermo. Macnamara and Spence collected the luggage, and Sula led them outside, into a long curved cloister lined with fluted pillars in the Dhai-ro style, where she took her first breath of free, cool Terran air. There had been rain, and the cool, humid air was heavy with the scent of grasses and flowers. All the species living under the Praxis bustled about the busy concourse, and Sula's nerves sang a warning as she saw Naxids scuttling among the throng. Centauroid, covered with beaded black scales, the Naxids zigzagged through the crowds as they sped about their errands.

Sula had killed Naxids with antimatter missiles, with bombs, with firearms, with improvised weapons. Even though the Naxids had been decisively defeated, Sula had spent too long a time killing them to be easy around them.

She tried to ignore her unease and stepped out from beneath the cloister. She looked up to see the two elevator cables foreshortening toward her from their vanishing point in the ring, both looking like the dark rain-streaked trunks of enormous trees.

She'd engaged a car and driver, and the Hunhao limousine, a lustrous and discreet maroon in color, pulled up on silent electric motors. The Lai-own driver stepped from his compartment, took his soft round cap off his feathery head, and rolled up the passenger door. Sula stepped inside and smelled hot coffee waiting in a flask.

They grew it here, didn't they? Normally, she preferred tea, but she thought perhaps she should try it.

Spense and Macnamara piled in after helping the driver with the luggage, and they all sampled the coffee. Sula found it too strong even after adding sugar, and returned the cup to its holder. The car crested a hill and the towers of Nairobi were revealed, all tinged red with the setting sun. Though the towers were grand enough, they seemed insignificant next to the sky-climbing elevator cables.

Sula was unimpressed by Nairobi during the two days she spent there. It was a large imperial city, rich with the trade going to and from orbit, and with a population drawn from every world of the empire and every corner of Earth. Those Dhai-ro pillars at the ground station had been only a foretaste of the city's style. Dhai-ro had been fashionable about the time of Earth's conquest, and when Nairobi had started to expand after the construction of the elevator, it had been built uniformly in the then-current style. Afterward, Nairobi had standardized on Dhai-ro as the style for all construction—unlike, say, Zanshaa, where every conceivable style was on view. Dhai-ro had faded in and out of fashion over the centuries and now seemed quaint, giving the city an old-fashioned, backwater air entirely at odds with its cosmopolitan population all hustling to make money.

Most disappointing, Sula decided, was that there seemed so little of old Earth there. Nairobi didn't seem Terran but rather a provincial copy of a bigger, better city somewhere else. There was a small museum featuring the bones and stone tools left by the prehistoric inhabitants of the nearby rift valley—all satisfyingly old, all satisfyingly prehuman—but otherwise, Sula's first taste of Earth was discouraging.

Her next stop was Constantinople, where she intended to pay a courtesy call on the imperial governor. That involved the supersonic train to Alexandria—where she hoped to spend more time later—followed by a ground-effect transport that roared across the Mediterranean in a blaze of white foam, dodging islands, until it finally slowed to enter the Dardanelles.

Sula spent some of the transit time doing her official work, forwarded by Parku on the ring, and the rest reading history and brooding on the landscape. The cities seemed no more or less venerable than cities on other worlds. The colors, she thought, were all wrong, beginning with the blue sky and the bright white light. She'd grown used to the deep green sky of Zanshaa and the planet's more subtle coloration.

It was during the passage of the Dardanelles that she received a call from Lieutenant-Captain Koridun. Sula was wearing her undress uniform—uniforms made wardrobe choices easier—and was able to receive the call on the communications unit woven into her left tunic sleeve.

"Yes?" she said. "Do you have your prisoner?"

Koridun's face appeared on the chameleon-weave display. "No, my lady, it was a case of mistaken identity." Sibilants hissed around her fangs, more than adequately conveying disgust. "The Palermo authorities completely bungled it."

"I'm sorry you wasted your trip."

"Unfortunate, but necessary," Koridun said. She made a visible effort, and her diction improved. "I wonder, lady commandant, if I may beg a favor."

"What do you need?" Offhandedly, expecting a request for a few days' leave.

"I wonder if you are still planning to pay a call on the lord governor?"

"I am."

Koridun hesitated, her tongue pressed to her foreteeth, and then spoke. "I wonder if it might be possible to beg an introduction."

Sula restrained a smile. Koridun's trip to the planet's surface was now explained—it made little sense for a lieutenant-captain to make the long journey merely in order to drag some crouchback to jail, but if the expedition could be combined with an introduction that might lead to patronage or advancement, then it would be well worth Koridun's time.

Sula approved of enterprise on the part of her subordinates. She saw no real reason to deny the request.

"I will be happy to provide the introduction," she said, "if you can be in Constantinople by tomorrow evening."

"I'll arrange transport. Thank you, my lady."

"I'll see you tomorrow."

Sula had no sooner blanked the screen than another

message came through, this time from Parku on the ring. His gray, expressionless face appeared on the display, a strip of dead skin hanging like an icicle from between his round, blank eyes.

"The new contract from the Manado Company has arrived," he said in his usual sonorous tones. "I am forwarding it to you for your approval and signature."

"Send it to the Office of the Judge Martial for review."

"It's just come from there, lady commandant. The contract passed review."

"Right, then. I suppose you may as well send it along."

So, it seemed that it *was* legal to rent Fleet docking facilities to private companies. Not that this had ranked high on Sula's list of concerns.

"Have you discovered anything more about the Manado Company?"

"Very little. Ownership is obscure, but the chief operating officer of the company is a Lord Peltrot Convil." Which was a Daimong name, not that this signified one thing or another.

"Any idea where the *Manado*'s been going on its missions? It has big antimatter engines; the flares should be easy to detect."

"I checked." A pained note entered Parku's tone. "*Manado* goes out *very* far, well past Neptune and into the Kuiper Belt. No one else ever goes to that quarter—there are no habitations, no mining ventures, nothing in that area at all. We could see their engine flares, but only if we have a detector pointing that way, and we never do, because there's never been any reason to look."

Sula rapped her knuckles on the arm of her chair in frustration. "Clearly, they've found *something*," she said.

"Yes, my lady."

"Keep looking."

"Of course, my lady."

And in the meantime, Sula thought, she'd wade through the dozens of pages that comprised the lease agreement, all in the hope that it might render some information.

Not that she thought it would.

"You are a celebrated war hero," said the lord governor. "Decorated." He nodded at the medals on Sula's dress tunic. "You destroyed those enemy ships at Magaria."

Actually, she'd destroyed enemy ships at Magaria *twice*, but Sula wasn't about to spoil a compliment by correcting it.

"You raised an army and captured the High City," the governor continued. "And despite your celebrity, you find yourself on Terra. I confess it surprised me."

"I won the war without permission," Sula said. "The credit was supposed to go to someone else. In fact, it *did* go to someone else."

The governor took a moment to process this. "That explains much," he decided.

Lord Moncrieff Ngeni was elderly and he moved with a degree of care, but it was difficult to tell his exact age. Terrans could live well past a hundred with the proper treatments, and Lord Moncrieff could clearly afford those. He could also afford cosmetic work: his dark-skinned face was as smooth and unlined as that of an infant, and only his aged, wrinkled hands hinted at his true age. His hair, unnaturally black, fell in tight waves over his collar, and he wore an equally black goatee that looked as if it properly belonged on the villain of a melodrama.

The grand purple robes of his office, with their gold and scarlet brocade, seemed a little too large for him. He spoke with a gentle voice, as if speaking loudly was too taxing for him.

Sula decided he was at least ninety.

"They want me out of the way while they write their official histories," Sula said. "So, here I am."

Lord Moncrieff gazed at Sula with mild eyes. "You're very outspoken."

Sula shrugged. "What I say doesn't matter. What *they* say matters a lot."

"Ah," said the lord governor. "Zanshaa." As if that said it all.

Lord Moncrieff was pleased to inquire how Sula had come to be given such an obscure assignment, but Sula decided not to ask the same question of the governor. She could guess how Lord Moncrieff had ended up there. Terra was the sort of place where careers went to die, and presumably Lord Moncrieff had been a disappointment to somebody, or a whole series of somebodies, and had been shuffled offstage with the sort of promotion that no one actually wanted.

Terra was a backwater. It possessed only a single wormhole gate, the one the Shaa had used when they sent in their conquering fleet, and commerce was restricted to that single access point. Worlds with thriving economies generally had many more useful wormhole gates, each of which led to other inhabited worlds, each offering the possibility of trade. In the Terran system, ships would arrive, stop, turn around, and go back, generally carrying more than they had brought. Billions of humans had left Earth over the centuries, moving up the giant elevator cables to board ships that would carry them to worlds of greater opportunity.

Earth had been the loser in the wormhole lottery.

Which was why it was a dead end, and a place for dead-end careers, like those of Sula and Lord Moncrieff.

"Speaking of history," said Lord Moncrieff, "I gather from one of your transmissions that you are interested in the history of Terra?"

"Yes," she said. "Very much."

"You must allow me to show you the view from my office. You might find the sight interesting."

The Palace of the Governor was in the heart of Constantinople, built over what had once been the palace of the caesars, and shambled from the heights of the city down to the waterfront at the Sea of Marmara. It was an eye-catching building, faced with porphyry polished to the color of fresh blood, and featuring cogged arches, niches with statues of Shaa administrators, plaques with quotations from the Praxis, and towers crowned by completely round domes, as if someone had set a cannonball atop each spire.

The style wasn't Terran. Sula wasn't sure that she had seen a single building in the local style, whatever that was.

The Lord Governor Ngeni had received her in his private apartments, and he led her up a marble stairway on which ran a plush waterfall of carpet the same color as the governor's robes. They walked down a corridor cluttered with trophies, old flags, and the busts of long-forgotten officials, to a private door that opened to Lord Moncrieff's thumbprint.

The lord governor kept the lights off—Sula had the impression of a massive desk, of mirrors, and of the odor of lemon polish—and then Sula followed the governor to a broad window that looked down on a long, narrow park.

"That is the racetrack of the old emperors," Lord Moncrieff said. "The actual racetrack is still there, though well buried—and there are those towery things."

"Obelisks."

"Yes. One of them is from Egypt, and the other, ah"—he gestured vaguely—"isn't."

"What did the emperors race?" Sula asked.

"Oh." Lord Moncrieff hesitated. "I don't think the emperors actually raced; I believe they just . . . presided."

"Ah."

"And it was chariots that raced, pulled by horses. Tens of thousands watched. I've seen some art about it . . . somewhere." He pointed through another window. "Beyond the racetrack is what's left of Hagia Sofia, after the earthquake a couple thousand years ago. The bits still standing aren't very interesting, but there's a museum with artifacts and a virtual reconstruction. Almost as good as the real thing—though of course, if you want the version that shows the religious art that was there at one time, you have to get clearance." Lord Moncrieff looked at her and smiled benignly. "I'll make the necessary arrangements, if you like."

"Yes," she said. "Thank you." She frowned down the long track of the racecourse to the vaguely discerned piles of masonry at the far end. "They haven't rebuilt it?"

Lord Moncrieff sighed. "We are in an earthquake zone. The government didn't tear down the antique buildings; that was the planet itself. There was a big mosque right over there"—he pointed at a gray, bunker-like building that seemed to exist perpetually within its own shadow—"named after Sultan Ahmet, who still gives his name to the district. The dome fell in a quake, and the rest was demolished to put up the Transport Council building. Very ugly; you're lucky you can't see it properly." He turned to her with a vague smile. "If you want to see a mosque, there's the Suleyman, fairly well preserved. I believe it's representative."

"Thank you. I'll be sure to visit."

"It's a concert hall now. And down below somewhere . . ." He flicked fingers in the direction of the floor. "There's a mosaic floor from the old palace."

"Which old palace is that?"

"Belonged to some caesar or other, I suppose. It's a good ways down, in a subbasement. I've never seen it, but I'll have Doctor Dho-ta take you down."

Some caesar or other. Sula felt herself vibrating with frustration. She wanted to grab some keys and charge down to the basement to view the ancient floors on which the Byzantine emperors had walked.

Governor of the whole planet, she thought, *and he can't take an interest in the artifacts under his own feet.*

"Who is Doctor Dho-ta?" Sula asked.

"He's head of Heritage and Artifacts. I invited him to dine with us tonight, since you're so interested in history and so on."

"Thank you. That was thoughtful."

There was a chime from somewhere in the lord governor's robes, and then a pause while Lord Moncrieff searched his pockets for his hand comm. He glanced at the screen, then stuffed the comm back in a pocket.

"Your Captain Koridun is here," he said. "Shall we join her?"

"It was very good of you to include her in the party."

The lord governor shrugged. "We have a Torminel chef on staff. Might as well give her some employment, eh?"

Koridun had arrived in dress uniform of tunic and trousers of viridian green, with two rows of silver button. Tufts of fur splayed out between her cuffs and her immaculate white gloves. Sula assumed there were hidden cooling units in her ensemble to prevent overheating.

Also in the party were Lady Alkan, the governor of

Constantinople; her consort, who seemed supremely bored and rarely spoke; a Cree actor of some local standing; and Lady Amelia Singh, Lord Moncrieff's wife. As chemically blond as Lord Moncrieff was sable, and with skin so taut that Sula thought she could bounce a rubber ball off it, Lady Amelia was an experienced hostess and managed to keep everyone in the conversation—everyone except Lady Alkan's husband, anyway.

Sula recognized the dinner service as Vigo hard-paste with a geometric design. She found herself seated across the dining table from Dr. Dho-ta and was vaguely surprised that an authority on Terran antiquities was a Laiown. He was middle-aged, having lost the feathery, dark juvenile hair on the sides of his flat head, and the peg teeth in his muzzle bore the stains of the inhaled dy-chi intoxicant.

At table, the intoxicants were more conventional. Somewhat to the lord governor's surprise, Sula declined the local wine offered to the Terrans and was served sparkling pomegranate juice. Koridun, like most Torminel, preferred to drink methanol, which was poisonous to humans. The Cree drank anything that was put in front of him, and Dho-ta, for whom any form of alcohol was fatal, instead took thu-thu in the form of pastilles placed at his elbow by a thoughtful servant.

The result was that Sula was the only completely sober person at the dinner. But then, she was used to that.

"We were discussing the Suleyman mosque," Lord Moncrieff said to Dho-ta. "I expect you know more about it than I do."

"It was built by one of the great Ottoman sultans," Dho-ta said. "Known as 'the Lawgiver' to his own people, though surprisingly his enemies called him 'the Magnificent.' His military and cultural achievements were considerable." His stained teeth clacked in thought. "His tomb was destroyed in an earthquake centuries ago, but I can send you a monograph about its excavation, if that would interest you."

"Thank you," Sula said. "I'd enjoy it."

"The fire damage to the concert hall has been repaired," Dho-ta added. "It's improved, if anything."

Lord Moncrieff saw Sula's questioning look and said, "A few years ago, an incident. Someone set himself on fire in there, and the fire spread."

"A fanatic," Dho-ta said. He shifted in the special chair that cradled his keel-like breastbone. "He wanted to return the mosque to its original religious function—not to Islam, curiously, but to something else, one of those syncretic cults that keep popping up."

"These people are Moncrieff's special burden," Lady Amelia said.

The lord governor gave a sigh. "There's something about Terra that creates cultists," he said. "Narayanists, Christians, Gnostics, Muslims, Manicheans, Rivolean Mandaeists, *and* Orgonic Mandaeists." He sighed and sipped his wine. "I can't say I much care what a person chooses to think, but they *will* preach in public, and they *will* get arrested and condemned, and the appeal *will* end up on my desk." He raised his hands in a gesture of helplessness. "Those who are insane I can have committed, but the rest are clearly in violation of the Praxis, and I have no choice but to approve their torture and execution."

Lady Alkan sniffed. "If only they *all* had the good taste to set themselves on fire."

Dho-ta turned to Sula. "That's why Jerusalem had to be leveled right to the bedrock," he said. "There was so much unrest there. And that's why the authorities took that rock from Mecca and sent it to some museum of cult artifacts on Preowyn."

"That just exported the problem," said Lady Amelia.

Lord Moncrieff gave his gentle smile. "But, my dearest, that means it's no longer *my* problem. One of my esteemed colleagues can sign the warrants, and at least some of the cultists will leave me in peace."

A servant whisked away Sula's plate, a second whisked away crumbs, and a third whisked a new course in front of her. The odor of singed flesh rose in her senses. She picked up her fork.

Lady Amelia guided the conversation away from the subject of cultists. Sula waited another two courses before bringing up a different martyr.

"I had the honor of commanding your cousin, Pierre, in the war," she said to Lord Moncrieff. "I imagine he *was* your cousin, yes?"

"Something like that," said the lord governor. "PJ—" He turned to the others and added an aside. "We called him PJ. He was an ornament to the family."

Sula smiled privately. *Ornament* was apt, for the amiable young man whose primary function in life had been decorative.

Lord Moncrieff turned to Sula. "We were a bit surprised, really, to hear he'd become such a hero."

"I used him to gather intelligence. He was so well connected that he could find out anything going on in the High City. But what he really wanted to do was fight, and so on the day we stormed the acropolis, he took up arms and got killed." She remembered the delightful, ridiculous PJ, and the joy that blazed from his face as she finally gave him permission to take part in military action.

She also remembered him dead, his hands still clenched on the rifle that hadn't fired a single shot, and an expression on his face of wistful surprise.

"He was very brave," Sula said. "I liked him."

"I'm sure he was fortunate to have you as a friend," Lord Moncrieff said.

Lady Amelia turned her sharp nose toward her husband. "He'd just been married to that Martinez woman, wasn't he?" she said. "After the first one ran off?"

PJ had loved his first Martinez fiancée, Sempronia, apparently unaware that the arrangement had been an alliance of convenience between the Martinez family and his own and that no feelings of affection were expected or necessary. When she'd run off with a secret lover, he'd not only suffered a broken heart but had been packed into a hasty marriage with Sempronia's older sister.

"Yes," Sula said. "That's what happened."

Loving a Martinez, as Sula knew to her cost, was a hazardous business.

"I imagine PJ didn't have much to live for after that," Lady Amelia said.

Nor did I, Sula thought. She had done her best to get herself killed, and failed, and instead ended up ruling a planet.

And though what Lady Amelia said was perfectly true, Sula felt she ought to correct the record. She preferred not to leave PJ Ngeni in such a hopeless light.

"He was brave," she insisted. "He stayed behind to fight. Almost all the important Peers fled and took their treasures with them, but he was willing to stand up against the invaders. With no training at all, unlike so many of those who just ran away."

Lady Amelia seemed not to appreciate the disparagement of her class.

"Peers fought," she said. "Many were killed."

"In the Fleet, yes," Sula said. "Peers make up most of the officers, and of course they were stationed on warships and couldn't run away. But Zanshaa? None of the first rank died there. By the end, I was the only Peer in the army."

"Wasn't there another Peer?" asked Koridun. She dabbed blood from her chin with a napkin. "Someone who was appointed governor?"

Sula felt her lips pucker at the sour memory. "Trani Creel was never in the army. She spent the war hiding in the country, then emerged after the fighting was over. She outranked me"—Sula shrugged—"so Fleet Commander Tork saw fit to appoint her governor." She turned to Lord Moncrieff. "She complained about the poor quality of her rations during the war. I complained about the shortage of bullets to fire at the enemy."

Lord Moncrieff smiled appreciatively. Lady Amelia gave Sula a quizzical look, and Sula could almost see her keen social antennae delicately probing the atmosphere. "I do not know any Lady Trani Creel," she said. "Not a prominent family, surely. Are you sure she was really governor of Zanshaa?"

"For only a few days," Sula said.

"She was murdered, was she not?" asked Koridun. She'd lost control of her diction, and the words lisped through her fangs.

Sula gave her subordinate an annoyed look. "She was killed in a riot," Sula said. "Lady Trani made the mistake of threatening a unit of the army, and . . ." She shrugged again. "They were all armed and, by then, used to killing."

In fact, Trani Creel had been killed at Sula's suggestion, by people she could trust to do the job. She'd had no intention of letting her work be undone by a fatuous, cowardly incompetent who would probably have only got herself killed sooner or later anyway.

"There was an investigation that identified the killers," Sula said.

"Were they ever caught?" lisped Koridun.

Sula turned to her. She supposed these were reasonable questions for a security officer to ask, but Koridun's persistence was irksome.

"I don't know," she lied. "I left Zanshaa to join the Fleet."

In fact, she'd invented the accused killers, forging both the documents that proved their existence and the evidence against them. They hadn't been caught for the simple reason that they were pure fiction.

Though that wasn't the sort of thing one could say at a dinner party.

Dho-ta seemed to perceive the awkwardness of the topic, and he lifted one of his thu-thu pastilles and regarded it critically while he changed the subject. "Lady Sula," he said, "as you're so interested in antiquities, I would like to offer you a guide for your stay here. My assistant, Mr. Ratnasari, can call for you tomorrow. What time would be convenient?"

"I wouldn't want to be any trouble."

Dho-ta popped the pastille in his mouth. "You honor us with your interest in our work. It will be my pleasure to offer you any guidance you need."

Your pleasure, Sula thought, *but Ratnasari's labor.* But she was delighted by the offer, and smiled.

"Tenth hour, if that's all right."

"Certainly."

Sula settled into her chair with a growing satisfaction. Perhaps there was a point to these dinner parties after all.

Aziq Ratnasari was a native Terran, from the state of Pahang in Southeast Asia, and shorter than Sula, with even, sepia-colored skin. Cheerfully he took Sula to see the mosaics under the Palace of the Governor. They were a mixture of natural and mythological subjects—griffins, animals, a Green Man, children rolling hoops, hunters pursuing game, a man feeding a donkey—and even the mythological subjects were shown in ordinary, everyday poses, as if they were nothing to get excited about.

Sula *was* excited. She'd never seen anything like it. If the mosaics had any instructive or ideological purpose, it was completely obscure. They seemed intended simply to delight.

The mosaics were set in the floor of what had once been a sizeable room in the palace, but no one knew who had commissioned the floor or what the room had been used for. It was as if one of the caesars had just sent a message of joy into the future.

Ratnasari answered Sula's questions about Byzantium and its monuments as well as he could. When she asked if any of the hippodrome racetrack were visible, Ratnasari said not, but that you could get to that level of the city through some tunnels at the back end of the racecourse.

"A bit damp, though," he said. "You'll need waders."

"Where can we find waders?" Sula asked.

Ratnasari had the waders brought from his office along with flashlights, then led her to the Sphendone, the bulwark supporting the south end of the hippodrome, an enormous brickwork mountain of tortured irregular arches and the remains of other structures that had once adhered to the wall. The Sphendone seemed to be holding up all Sultanahmet, including the Palace of the Governor, and appeared to have undergone some kind of horrific geological process. There were arches that faced in different directions, stairs that led nowhere in particular, bricks that had been fused together by gravity and the ages, their courses tipped at alarming angles. All the arches had long ago been bricked up, and those bricks had been subjected to the same tortuous tectonic history as the rest.

"These arches were once identical," he said. "But a few thousand years of earthquakes and patching and reconstruction made each one unique." Waders squeaked as he led Sula up a narrow metal stair and through a battered steel door that opened to his thumbprint. Air wafting through the door smelled of time and cool water. He groped to his left, found an old-fashioned switch; Sula heard a clack and saw lights go on.

"Come in," said Ratsanari. Sula followed him into the chamber and stood on a metal bar grating poised above a long, curving, flooded corridor. Overhead wire strung floodlights together, and in the glare, the passages were filled either with brilliant light or deepest shadow.

Below the platform, still water formed a perfect mirror of the arches overhead, making the corridor seem far taller than it was.

Brick and more brick, damp and mossy, oozing nitre, courses as tempest-tossed as the ocean. In the silence Sula could hear the throb of her own heart.

"I'll go first," Ratnasari said. "I'm shorter, and if I fall in a pit and my waders fill, I know how to escape."

"Very good." Sula already loved the place but preferred it not be her tomb.

"This was used as a mosque once, then converted to a cistern." He waved his arms apologetically. "It's proved difficult to drain."

Sula turned on her light and followed Ratnasari down into the clear water. It came up past her knees, and waves spread from her legs to lap against the ancient bulwark. Her skin prickled with cold. Fish darted in and out of her flashlight beam.

The ancient walls were spangled by dancing light reflecting off the water. Sula followed Ratnasari down the long curve that formed the end of the racecourse. Apparently, chariots needed a lot of room to turn. Ratnasari spoke cheerfully about the history of the hippodrome, built originally by Septimius Severus, enlarged and improved by Justinian, and subsequently sacked by rioters, Crusaders, Mamelukes, and neglect. "Justinian also suppressed the Nika riots," he said. "You've heard about them?"

"Yes, of course." Justinian was the sort of Terran ruler of whom the Shaa conquerors could approve. Slaughtering thirty thousand dissidents with primitive weapons was an act which the Shaa could only admire, and the deed was celebrated in the approved Earth histories.

"Not bad, considering the limitations of the technology," Sula judged. She considered the antimatter missiles that had fallen on Petrograd, Cape Town, Mumbai, Shanghai, Los Angeles, New York, and so many of Earth's other great cities.

"Though of course," she added, "the Great Masters put Justinian to shame."

"The Shaa were perfection itself when it came to upholding the strictures of the Praxis," said Ratnasari. Sula gave him a sharp look, both at the possibility of irony and the fact that the words sounded familiar.

"From the eulogy given the last Shaa," Ratnasari said helpfully.

"I missed the funeral," Sula said. "I was on duty." Guarding the terminal of a space elevator, in case the passing of the Great Masters led to despair, anarchy, and violence.

Which, against the odds, it had not. At least, not *then*.

Another hour was spent splashing around in the corridor, and then they hauled themselves out of the chilly water and returned to the warmth and life of the city.

"Where next?" Sula asked.

"Well." Ratnasari offered a brilliant smile. "We already have the waders."

"Then we'd better wade."

A Byzantine cistern had recently been discovered in Edirnekapı, millennia old and forgotten for most of those thousands of years. The place had never been open to the public, hadn't been fully explored, and there were no lights but what Sula and Ratnasari brought with them. The place was magical, and Sula wandered through cool water thigh-deep while the light of her flash gilded the drops of water that rained from the ceiling. The pillars that supported the distant brick arches were all different, some of elaborately patterned marble, and were a contrast to the utilitarian brickwork of the ceiling vaults.

Next was the Cistern of a Thousand and One Columns, which didn't require waders because it was dry and filled with small shops. Ratnasari suggested tea and snacks. They sat in a cafe, Sula looked at the porcelain and found it undistinguished, and they discussed Earth history for a long, civilized hour. She was surprised at how many gaps existed in her education.

"It's not surprising," Ratnasari said. "The Shaa conquered an empire, and so they favored the bits of Terran history that mirrored their own experience. So, if we're taught anything about Earth history at all, it's usually about the Egyptians, Chinese, Persians, Romans, and so forth, right up to the Russian and British empires. Other histories were neglected or sometimes suppressed."

"Such as?"

"The history of religion is pretty well kept out of the standard texts. You need special permission to study the ancient cults—though of course, if you have the right academic qualifications, permission isn't that hard to get."

"You have such permission?"

"No, that's not my field." He offered a shy smile. "I'm more of a specialist in government—it's surprising how many forms of government the old Terrans came up with."

"Such as?"

"Corporatocracy, where a country is directly ruled by a profit-seeking corporation."

"Making a profit seems a narrow basis for government."

"At one point, the British East India Company ruled all of India, and the Dutch East India Company ruled the Indonesian archipelago. They issued their own coin, had their own armies, and possessed the right to declare war. They went on for centuries."

Sula thought she spotted the flaw in this arrangement.

"What was the responsibility of the corporation to the population they governed?"

"None. Only to the stockholders." Ratnasari smiled. "The India companies imposed their rule on the population by treaty or conquest—of course, the conquered people were far away from the stockholders, oceans away in a period when it took a long time to cross an ocean."

"So, all the stockholders knew of the companies' actions was when the dividends arrived."

"Or *didn't* arrive. The India Companies' rule was based on monopoly, and once that monopoly was compromised, they failed, and the parent governments had to step in and rule directly."

Sula sampled an eggplant dish. "In what other imaginative ways were our ancestors governed?"

Ratnasari mentioned diarchies, triarchies, and tetrarchies, which Sula thought useful insofar as the rulers could check each other, and timocracies, where honor was the primary virtue, and the rulers tended to come from the military.

"A recipe for catastrophe," Sula said. "In my experience, most high-ranking military can't even command their own units, let alone a state."

Laughter might have been dangerous, and Ratnasari controlled his, but there was still a glimmer of amusement in his eyes. "I defer to your superior experience, my lady." He waved a hand. "If the commanders can't run things, you could try demarchy, in which officials are chosen randomly from a list of eligible citizens. Most posts in ancient Athens were filled that way. It's a preventative against corruption."

Sula couldn't see the point. "Why would random people be less prone to corruption than anyone else?" she asked.

"Fewer long-standing relationships with corrupting influences, I suppose."

"Corrupting influences have a way of finding their way to those with power. Besides, I thought the old Athenians had mob rule."

Ratnasari considered this, then spoke carefully. "That is the classic accusation against democracy, that a mob would vote unwisely or rule through violence. You would know better than I if the same accusations might be made against our Convocation."

Sula sipped her tea and contemplated the possibility that she might be talking with a subversive. On the basis of that last sentence alone, she could probably have Ratnasari arrested and killed.

Not that Ratnasari wasn't *right*. The Convocation's decisions in the late war had been disastrous and veered between reckless delusion and utter cowardice.

Plus, of course, they ruled through violence, as any well-bred mob might do.

"In fact," Ratnasari added, "most violent mobs were historically in service to those in power."

Sula was surprised. "Why would someone in power need a mob?"

"To enforce their rule through terror and violence. Police are supposed to have scruples and obey the law, but mobs don't have to—and they provide a degree of deniability to those whose interests they serve." Ratnasari poured strong black tea for the both of them. "The exception is during periods of actual revolution, when the authority of government is absent or compromised, as in the Nika riots we just mentioned. *Then* you find mobs acting against the established order. But under normal conditions, governments can suppress citizens who challenge them—if they couldn't do something as simple as that, they could scarcely survive as governments. So, any group of citizens who appear out of control and cause chaos are most likely working for the authorities, whether they know it or not."

Sula considered this as she poured honey into her tea. What Ratnasari said was reflected in her own career—she had led her own army in support of a government that she distrusted and disliked.

Of course, it was easier to support the legitimate government when it was the rebels who were trying to kill her.

And she had also employed a mob of sorts against Trani Creel, the governor whose assassination she had arranged. Which might have been an attack on the established order, except that the results were in favor of a previous order she had established herself.

This was growing confusing. Sula decided that it was futile to try to fit her actions into anyone's categories but her own.

Sula sipped her tea and said nothing. Ratnasari filled the silence. "If these anachronistic political arrangements interest you, you might be interested in Democracy Club."

A wave of pure blazing paranoia flamed through Sula. Ratnasari was not only voicing subversive ideas a short distance from Earth's seat of government, but he was also trying to recruit Sula for some kind of political club. Which meant not that he was some kind of evangelist for an alternate political system, but that he was an *agent provocateur,* someone who intended to compromise Sula with the authorities or get her killed.

"I'm not very interested in political questions," she said.

"Oh." Ratnasari was surprised. "I must have been unclear. Democracy Club doesn't *advocate* democracy—that would of course be absurd for anyone living under the perfection of the Praxis. No, instead we *re-create* democracy as a method of understanding the past."

Sula was still wary. "Perhaps you'd better explain," she said.

"Well." Ratnasari's fork dug into a pastry. "You're familiar with re-creationist groups, yes? People who dress up as people from history and reenact the past?"

"No."

"You don't have them on Zanshaa?" Ratnasari seemed disappointed.

"Not that I know of. Unless you count costume parties."

Ratnasari was thoughtful. "Of course, the Shaa established the Praxis as something eternal and unchanging, so there would be no point in re-creating the past—it would be just like the present, yes? But here on Earth, we have thousands of years of history before the Shaa appeared, so sometimes, groups of people try to re-create aspects of the past in order to better understand them—how life was lived with primitive technology, or how people organized themselves, or how battles were fought—"

"*Battles?*" Sula said. "You fight *battles?*" Ratnasari had swerved from subversion to gang warfare.

"Well," Ratnasari said, "no one actually gets killed.

They fire blanks or whatever, or fight with dummy swords. But the uniforms and the tactics and so on are authentic."

Sula's military experience had included seeing her commander die in antimatter fire, watching her comrades tortured to death on video, standing by in helpless anguish while her lover died of a wound that the doctor somehow hadn't managed to locate in time.... She couldn't work out exactly how Ratnasari's dummy combat was *authentic,* not without people being hacked or blown to bits, without the blood of children running in the streets, without thousands of the Fleet's finest annihilated *even on the atomic level,* and all in the blink of an eye....

Sula made an effort to unclench her fists. "Without death," she said, as mildly as she could, "you rather miss the point." Without real death, she thought, it was all just a costume party.

"I don't really know about those groups," Ratnasari said quickly. "I specialize in government."

"Ah. Right."

"In fact, Democracy Club is meeting in a few days. Perhaps you would consider attending, if you're interested."

Sula made an effort to be civil. "I don't think my career would be enhanced by practicing a system forbidden by the Praxis."

"Oh! That's all right!" Ratnasari grinned. "We have permission from Lord Governor Ngeni to perform historical experiments. I even send him abstracts of all our sessions."

Sula looked at Ratnasari with increased respect. He seemed to have covered himself rather well.

Then she noticed, out of the corner of her eye, three Daimong members of the Legion of Diligence enter the cafe, and she stiffened. Despite their chiming talk, the pale expressionless faces floating above the black uniforms looked like an ominous, spectral visitation from a world of ghosts.

The Legion of Diligence was the dreaded corps charged with investigating crimes against the Praxis, and were known for their rigor, efficiency, and brutality. It was the Legion who had investigated and killed Caro Sula's parents, and if anyone reported the conversation that Sula and Ratnasari had just had, it was the Legion who would investigate whether or not a capital crime had just been committed.

Sula finished her tea and placed the cup in its saucer. "Let's look at Hagia Sofia, shall we?"

The ruins of the great basilica had a broad-shouldered majesty that hinted at the state power that had created such a vast interior space in an era when the most advanced tools were dividers, squares, and plumb bobs.

Sula learned new words like "exonarthex," viewed more repurposed pagan pillars lying in rows or supporting half-ruined structures, and explored the re-created virtual basilica from the viewing room of a nearby museum. Lord Moncrieff had given permission for her to view the cult art that had once saturated the interior: Christ Pantokrator on the ventral surface of the great dome, gazing down at the congregation with an expression of faint concern; saints and emperors and virgins on nearly every other surface; and eerie cherubim on the pendentives beneath the dome, solemn faces wreathed in sets of multiple wings. Almost all done in mosaic against a background of gold tiles that glowed like a brilliant sunrise in the light of the high windows.

Below the great dome were the Ottoman additions: more brilliant tiles in a rainbow of color, the intricate screen of the Sultan's loge, the giant wheel-like chandeliers, and the great medallions inscribed with the names of Muhammad and his early followers. In the virtual basilica, it was possible to observe the building at different stages, to view Justinian's original structure, watch in turn subsequent modifications, the various reconstructions, the additions of the Ottomans, the last restoration under the Shaa before the earthquake ruined all their labor. Sula spent half the afternoon looking at the building and found herself thinking about Justinian, who had slaughtered thirty thousand of his own citizens, sent his armies rampaging on campaigns of conquest throughout the Mediterranean, then built this magnificent monument to himself, or his god, or both.

She'd seen the Great Refuge, where the Shaa conquerors lived out their long lives, and the Couch of Eternity, where their ashes were stored, and though each building was monumental, neither could be described as inspiring—unless, possibly, you were one of the Shaa. They were labyrinths, almost like office buildings, with no great open spaces, no attempt to inspire the imagination, no originality or innovation. The Great Refuge was a place for work. The Couch of Eternity was a place where the Shaa were laid to rest in disciplined, orderly rows.

To the Shaa, all the great questions had already been answered. It remained only to carry out the plan that had been decided centuries ago, then die.

It wasn't until she left the museum and looked up into the sky, where the antimatter ring arched high above the world, and she thought, *Well, maybe the Shaa built some impressive things, after all.*

———

Sula spent three days in Constantinople, viewing monuments with Ratnasari, then got back on the ground-effect transport and roared back to Egypt, where she was guided by one of Ratnasari's colleagues. The Giza pyramids had been restored some centuries in the past by Lady Camille Umri, who had re-sheathed the structures in the brilliant white limestone in which they had first been dressed. She had also re-created some of the associated buildings, and was in the middle of restoring the pyramids of Dahshur when her family's fortune ran out, and she ended in a hospital ward under the impression she was Hatshepsut.

Sula thought the pyramids, unlike Hagia Sophia, were very much like something the Shaa might have built, as a monument to the Fundamental Gravity of the Praxis or the Incontrovertible Perfection of Geometry, or something equally dogmatic. Most of the Egyptian monuments seemed as programmatic as anything the Shaa had built, and seeing the pyramids beneath the arch of the antimatter ring didn't seem a contradiction at all.

She reported these thoughts to Cousin Goojie, who was still stuck in her long deceleration burn. Caro Sula's best friend was proving a good sounding board for her ideas, possibly because Goojie had nothing to do on her transport but listen to Sula's dispatches.

"You know," Goojie said in response, "it never occurred to me that even on Earth, there would be anything different from what we see everywhere else in the empire." Her green eyes narrowed. "I don't remember you being at all interested in history. When did you change?"

Sula felt a warning finger touch her spine. Caro Sula's interest in clothes, alcohol, and drugs had left little time for any other hobbies—so perhaps a deep interest in and knowledge of Earth history might seem suspicious to anyone who knew Caro in person.

But there had been a great many years since Goojie had seen Caro in the flesh.

"I got interested in history when I left Zanshaa," Sula said in her return message, "and saw how different everything was from what I'd seen in the capital."

If that sounded odd to Goojie, she didn't mention it in her response.

Sula returned to Constantinople on the night that Democracy Club was scheduled to meet. She would have begged off if Ratnasari hadn't shown up in person to take her to the meeting—she decided she owed him for the splendid time she'd had splashing through ancient tunnels beneath the city, and agreed to join him.

The club met in a small lecture room in the supremely ugly Transport Council building, built over what had been the Sultan Ahmet Mosque. Sula counted sixteen people, of whom a dozen were Terran and the rest divided between Lai-own and Torminel.

Half seemed to have brought takeout dinner with them, and the scent of grilled proteins wafted through the room. Most of the participants were dressed in anachronistic costumes featuring dull colors and eccentric neckware, presumably appropriate to whatever democracy they were supposed to represent. Ratnasari introduced Sula to his co-enthusiasts, and to her slight embarrassment, they applauded her.

She took a position to one side while the umpire, a Miss Çetinkaya, explained the night's exercise. The participants were playing the roles of the city council and the mayor of Milwaukee, Wisconsin, United States of America. They were meeting to discuss the budget, which had already been passed but which required modification due to a predicted twenty percent shortfall, an economic downturn, a large corporation moving its headquarters to another city, and bad weather resulting in less grain being shipped through the port.

Ratnasari, taking a seat next to Sula, explained that the United States had been a prosperous democratic republic, in which citizens elected others to represent them on the city council and other civic forums.

"I thought the United States was some kind of oligarchy based on religion."

"That, too."

The discussion among the hobbyists was prolonged,

embracing a wide variety of solutions, including raising taxes, cutting personnel, issuing bonds, charging more for use of city facilities . . . and by that point, Sula had stopped listening. Democracy, she decided, had to be the most idiotic form of government ever invented.

Why not just appoint someone to deal with the situation? If he succeeded, he would be rewarded, and if he met with disaster . . . and at that point, her imagination failed because those who failed in the empire were judged not by their actions but by the virtues of their ancestors. Those belonging to important families either continued in office, were promoted, or went on to other endeavors; and those with insufficiently grand connections were disgraced, dismissed, imprisoned, or executed. In any case, lines of responsibility were clear.

In Milwaukee, no single individual seemed to be in charge of anything, and so they argued interminably about things for which they had no personal responsibility. And most of them seemed to have very little practice at public speaking, so they meandered about the subject without ever quite getting to the point.

Sula relieved the tedium of the meeting by opening her sleeve display and planning the next stages of her journey, but she was distracted by a Terran woman across the room who was trying to attract her attention.

The woman was costumed in a severe dark gray skirt-suit, pale blouse, and a floppy dark strip of cloth tied around her neck. Her skin was a dark teak color, and her long hair a bright henna-red. She kept looking at Sula and grinning at her, nodding as if Sula was an old friend and should nod back.

Sula couldn't recollect seeing the woman before—that brilliant red hair would be something she'd remember—but then, she'd met a lot of people since she became a celebrity, and she supposed she couldn't recall them all. And possibly, she thought, the hair hadn't always been red.

Sula nodded, gave a little wave, and returned to her sleeve display. The woman's grin broadened and she returned the wave. Sula ignored her.

Eventually, the meeting driveled on to a conclusion, and a new budget passed by a narrow majority. Relieved beyond measure, Sula turned off her sleeve display, rose from her chair, and stretched.

"Did you enjoy that?" Ratnasari said. "Wasn't it interesting?"

"I had no idea our ancestors got up to such things," Sula said. No wonder they got themselves conquered, she thought, if all they did was engage in pointless debate while the Shaa missiles were heading for their cities.

The henna-haired woman bustled through the crowd

and appeared at Sula's elbow. "It's good to see you again," she said.

"Always a pleasure," Sula said. "But I'm afraid your name has slipped my mind."

"Adele Souka," the woman said.

Neither the name nor her appearance triggered any memory in Sula.

"What are you doing on Terra?" Sula asked.

Adele Souka was surprised by the question. "The same as when we last spoke. I'm working for Kantari Modulars."

Sula didn't know Kantari Modulars, either. She felt a vague, possibly apologetic smile creep over her face. "Very good," she said.

Adele Souka seemed puzzled. "You don't remember?" she said. "It was only—"

"Captain Sula! Captain Sula!" The new arrival was a tall, spindly Terran, pale, with a full beard, suede boots, a pinstripe suit that made him seem even taller than he was, and a full grin.

"I'm Jack Danitz," he said. A big baritone voice boomed from his narrow chest. "I was the council member who represented the Hmong neighborhood, you may remember."

"Of course," Sula said. She remembered the big baritone voice and wondered as well what a Hmong might be, but couldn't recall anything Danitz actually said, or whether it was useful.

"I belong to another club besides this one," said Jack Danitz. "We do military simulations."

"Ah. Hah," Sula said. She presumed Danitz probably fought in those bloodless battles that Ratnasari had mentioned.

"We've been meeting recently," Danitz continued, "and we've been refighting Second Magaria—and we can't seem to get it to come out the way it did in reality."

She blinked up at him. "How exactly—"

"Oh. We use a tactical computer simulation, like those used in Fleet exercises. The same software, actually, because some of our club members are well placed and were able to get ahold of an older version of actual Fleet software. And the armament and capabilities of the various ships are available in the public record, after all, so all the preparation needed was to plug the information into the program." His toothy grin broadened. "I've played *you*, commanding Light Squadron Seventeen in the van. But I keep getting killed."

Sula smiled inwardly. Sacrificing Light Squadron Seventeen had very clearly been part of Fleet Commander Tork's plan during the battle.

"We've fought the battle over and over," Danitz said. "Sometimes the loyalists win, sometimes the Naxids, but the one thing that's constant from one simulation to the next is that the van squadron is always annihilated." Danitz looked down at Sula in apparent delight. "And yet here you are!"

Sula threw out her arms, like an actor taking a bow. "Yet here I am," she agreed.

"And seven of your ships survived. Every time we refought the battle, the whole group was wiped out!"

"Sorry you got such a thrashing."

"We've worked on the problem for months!" Danitz proclaimed. "And we've done absolutely *ridiculous* amounts of research—" He pointed a narrow finger at her. "I probably know more about you than anyone besides yourself. All about your life, your family, that time you spent on Spannan before you went to the academy . . ."

Sula's heart lurched. A wave of heat flooded up her spine. If there was one thing she did *not* want researched, it was Caro Sula's time on Spannan.

"I don't think—think that sort of thing will help." She cursed the stammer that made her seem like a guilty idiot.

Danitz stepped closer, looming over her like one of the pillars of Karnak. Sula caught a whiff of underarm and exasperation. "*How did you do it*?" he demanded. "How did you preserve your command? We've all been cudgeling our brains and—"

Sula took a step back away from the towering figure, the roaring voice, the threatening finger wagging in her face, but found a desk directly behind her and her line of retreat blocked. Claustrophobia seized her chest with steel talons. She struggled to master her rising terror and strike back at this looming, clamorous nightmare.

Sula narrowed her eyes. "I'm not going to help you win your next game," she said. "That would give you an unfair advantage."

Danitz spluttered. "That's not what I meant!" he bellowed. "Look—you can come to our next meeting and take command of your squadron yourself. We could all refight the battle! We'd *love* to watch you! Learn from you!"

"If you ever work out how I did it," she said, "let me know." She turned to Ratnasari. "Could you possibly take me back to the lord governor's palace?" she asked. "It's been a long day." She looked over her shoulder at the assembled group. "Pleasant to meet you all." She gave a little wave to Adele Souka on her way out and received a melancholy, baffled look in response.

In the car, on her way to the hotel, while Ratnasari burbled on the subject of Democracy Club and all the exciting conclusions about Earth's past that could be drawn from the night's meeting, Sula's fear and claustrophobia turned to paranoia.

A whole *club,* she thought as she rubbed the pad of scar tissue on her right thumb, a whole *club* was investigating her. A club that included well-placed individuals with access to Fleet software and Fleet data. A whole club digging into every aspect of her life in hopes it would somehow reveal her tactics at Second Magaria, but could just as easily—could *more* easily—reveal her tactics on Spannan, when she had stepped into Caro Sula's identity.

As paranoia took hold, she began to wonder if Danitz had actually found out something and was trying to blackmail her in some incredibly clumsy way.

In any case, there was no point in staying to make herself a target.

"Pack up," she told Spence and Macnamara when she returned to her rooms. "We're leaving in the morning."

Who was she now? she wondered. The person who fled from a threat that might not even be real.

———

The next stop was Cappadocia, in central Anatolia, where Sula viewed the eerie hoodoo spires and monoliths of the local topography, and ordered a set of porcelain. She had gotten used to the more violent colors of Earth and ordered a pattern of tulips and pomegranates vivid with reds and blues and greens. It was too bright and brilliant and eye-catching for a formal dinner—she'd have to buy another set later—but it would be a delightful setting for a small, intimate dinner for friends.

Assuming she ever made any friends, of course.

Next was India, followed by China. Lord Moncrieff Ngeni kindly provided letters of introduction to the local authorities, and Dr. Dho-ta to historians and archaeologists, and so she was well received and feted and taken on special tours of the local monuments. The hospitality was flawless, but she felt a certain discontent with the historical banquet laid before her. Constantinople's problems were reproduced wherever she visited: what remained of Earth's unique civilizations had been subjected to earthquake, flood, war, accident, and above all to time. Much was reduced, lay in ruins, or had been built over by the universal culture of the Shaa. Some places had been reconstructed, as had the pyramids, but often the reconstructions seemed crude, or designed to please visitors rather than transmit Terran ideas and Terran cultural heritage.

Which, she realized, was exactly what the Shaas would have preferred. Genuine Terran ideas might be dangerous; administrators probably thought it far safer to build a harmless historical amusement park.

Years ago, when she was Earthgirl, she'd been in love with this place, with the epic stories of kings and queens and world-striding emperors she'd found in the histories, with the stories of eccentric scientists, poets, generals, and spies that she'd uncovered. She wondered now if she'd invented most of those stories herself out of a few sanitized facts culled from heavily censored histories, all combined with her desperate need to escape her own drear circumstances and enter a dazzling world filled with adventure and exoticism.

Maybe she'd been more desperate than she remembered.

———

She didn't neglect her work while she was traveling. A daily summary of events kept her informed. Documents came down from the dockyard, were viewed, signed, or sent back for redrafting. Some personnel were caught misbehaving, Koridun recommended punishment, and Sula confirmed Koridun's suggestions. A jurisdictional dispute was settled by Parku without Sula having to intervene.

"I've received several messages from the Manado Company, my lady," Parku told her. "They're eager to know when you're going to sign the contract allowing them use of the dockyard."

"I want to review it again," Sula said. She'd looked at it carefully and found it unobjectionable on the surface, but she still sensed something wrong with the arrangement, and she hesitated to confirm it.

"The last call came from Lord Peltrot Convil," Parku said.

"Who's he again?"

"Chief operating officer of the company, my lady."

Lord Peltrot had slipped Sula's mind, and she decided she might as well let him slip again. "Is their ship still in dock?"

"*Manado* departed five days ago, following provisioning. Their crew included two company officers sent out from Zanshaa."

What, Sula wondered, would bring two officers all the way from the capital?

"Do you have their names?"

Parku did. Judging by their names, one was Daimong, the other Lai-own.

"What were their titles?" Sula asked.

"Both were referred to as 'senior engineering staff.'"

"What exactly are they engineering?"

"The Manado Company makes little information available, but I found their names and credentials listed by their previous employers. One is a mining engineer and the other an ecologist who has consulted in the field of environmental systems for space habitats."

"Mining engineer," Sula repeated. She nodded to herself. "They've found something out there, haven't they? Resources they plan to dig out of a planetoid, or something."

"I think that is very likely, my lady."

"Keep *Manado* under observation. We don't want to lose it this time."

"Very good, my lady."

She spent the next two days in Xi'an, reviewing the treasures of Shihuangdi's tomb, and lost track of the Manado contract until she received a call from Lord Peltrot Convil himself.

"Lady Sula," he said, "I wonder when we might expect your signature on the agreement to use your dockyard."

Sula looked at the expressionless Daimong face on her sleeve display. To a Terran, Daimong often looked like someone struck by amazement or by horror—Lord Peltrot's appearance, with its round dark featureless eyes and open, fixed mouth, seemed set in an expression more akin to belligerence. His chiming voice was deep and bell-like.

"I'd like to review the contract one more time, Lord Peltrot," Sula said.

"My understanding is that the contract was approved by the Judge Martial, so there is no legal impediment."

"That's true. But I wish to—"

"I believe you're visiting Terra at present, Lady Sula."

Lord Peltrot's bell-like voice took on an insistent, clanging tone. "May I offer you hospitality at our headquarters at Manado so we can discuss the matter?"

"Where *is* Manado, Lord Peltrot?"

"On the island of Sulawesi."

Which, east of Borneo and straddling the equator, was near one of the elevator terminals for the antimatter ring, and therefore a practical place for a company engaged in space exploration to have its headquarters.

Sula considered the offer and decided she might as well accept. Seeing Lord Peltrot and touring the Manado Company's facility might give her a clue about why she felt uneasy about the Manado contract.

"I'm pleased to accept your invitation, Lord Peltrot," she said.

———

"I've finally docked," Goojie reported. "I walked straight into a meeting with the managers here on the ring, and since I had nothing to do on the ship but view their reports, I think I was pretty well prepared, and it went well."

"Congratulations," said Sula.

It was their first actual conversation, as opposed to recording messages for one another. The antimatter ring was close enough to the planet to permit something like normal dialogue, with the delay of less than second between a word spoken on the planet and its arrival on the ring.

"I'll be here another few days," Goojie continued, "and then I'll be ready to come down to the skyhook and start to explore the planet."

Sula was only moderately surprised. Peers were regularly appointed to positions where they weren't expected to do more than a modest amount of work—her own appointment as head of the dockyards being a prime example.

Still, she thought, she should perhaps express more surprise than she actually felt.

"Are you sure they can spare you this early?" she asked.

Goojie grinned. "Kan-fra's headquarters is in Quito, and there are branches of the company all over the planet. I'll be based in Quito and can decide to inspect any of the subsidiaries at any time." She laughed. "It's my proactive policy! I want to be involved in decisions on every level!"

"Congratulations," Sula said. "I wish *my* policy was as proactive as yours."

"You're in China now, yes? Where are you going next?"

"Manado, on Sulawesi."

"Yes? Is there good shopping there?"

Sula laughed. "I don't know. I'll be there for a meeting."

"I'm going to have to go down to the planet somewhere; it may as well be Sulawesi. Shall I meet you there, schedules permitting? Or shall I go on to my inspection tour in New Zealand first?"

"You're going to start in New Zealand? Why New Zealand?"

"The Arch of Macedoin. I've always wanted to see it."

Well, the Arch *was* on Sula's itinerary, though she hadn't planned to see it anytime soon. "New Zealand's a long distance from Manado," she pointed out. "Or anywhere, for that matter."

"I have access to a company aircraft. You can fly as my guest."

Which certainly seemed preferable to rattling across half the Pacific in a ground-effects craft. "Is there room for my two staff?" Sula asked.

"Servants, you mean? Of course."

It seemed only polite to try to reciprocate the hospitality. "I'll see if you can ride in the elevator's Fleet compartment as my guest."

Sula had a few days left in China, during which she visited a reconstructed Wall and some reconstructed pagodas, and also ordered the large porcelain dinnerware set suitable for her rank. Hard-paste, thin, beautifully pale, the hand-painted rim decorated with the Sula crescents and in the center the badge of the frigate *Confident,* her first—and probably last—actual command.

And then she surrendered to her weakness and bought four Jian tea bowls dating from the Song dynasty. They were not part of a set—*sets* did not survive thousands of years and the successive fall of empires—so each was unique, with a crackled black glaze described variously as "partridge-feather," "hare's fur," or "tea dust," depending on exactly how the glaze separated during cooling. The patterns were random but beautiful, and Sula could feel the ripple of the broken glaze against her fingertips when she caressed the cups. She had only to see them in the store to know exactly how she would display them in her tower office back on the ring.

She didn't want to think about how much of her money she'd spent on the cups.

Who was she now? A connoisseur, apparently.

Sulawesi's odd shape, with its four long, thin peninsulas spread out like the fingers of a lemur, disguised its considerable size, with more landmass than England. Manado was an enormous port on the northernmost peninsula through which the commerce coming up and down the skyhook was shipped to all of Asia, Australia, and the west coast of the Americas. Cargo ships the size of skyscrapers lay at the harbor's piers, their decks stacked with containers coming from as far away as Seizho, Zanshaa, or Arkhan-Dohg. Huge masts shaded the harbor, each capable of spreading vast viscose-thin sails so enormous and perfectly cut that they could propel the huge ships with efficiency so high that the engines would only be used if the wind died away completely.

Naxids scurried everywhere. They liked the equatorial heat as much as Torminel hated it. Sula reminded herself that the Naxids on Terra had never rebelled, that for the length of the war, they'd remained good citizens of the empire, but still she couldn't help but feel crosshairs on the back of her neck.

The tropical heat and humidity had Sula broiling in her dress uniform. She wished it featured cooling units like those in Koridun's rig.

Fortunately, she wasn't exposed to the heat for long: Macnamara drew the car up to a nondescript office building overlooking a shabby boatyard, and Lord Peltrot welcomed Sula and brought her into his climate-controlled office. She tucked her cap under one arm as she entered.

Peltrot was short and stocky, which hadn't been obvious from his video image. He had a forceful way of walking, with his chest and chin outthrust. He must have bathed very recently, because Sula didn't need to resort to whiffing the perfume she'd dabbed on her wrists and handkerchief.

The Manado Company offices were small and featured only a handful of employees working behind large displays to the incessant sound of banging and clattering from the boatyard.

"Our personnel are scattered in ports throughout the empire," said Lord Peltrot. "That's where day-to-day decisions are made, so we don't need impressive offices. Our investors are interested in profits, not in ostentation."

Which made them unique among the rich people Sula knew. "Who *are* your investors?" she asked.

"We're privately held," Peltrot said. "I regret to say that's all confidential."

Sula peered over the shoulder of a Lai-own and saw that her display showed Terra stretched out in projection, with the paths of ships marked out on the blue water.

"You own seagoing ships as well as spaceships?" she said.

Peltrot gave a bright, affirmative chime. "Organizing one form of transport is very much like organizing another. It was convenient to acquire expertise during an expansion, and a shipping company was available. Just as we acquired the *Bombardment of Utgu* after the end of the late conflict."

Sula decided not to pursue the awkward question of how the Manado Company had obtained a warship. That was all well before her time, and she wouldn't get the real answer, anyway.

But the knowledge of that irregularity—a warship badly needed in the Fleet somehow finding itself in civilian hands—was enough to make her uneasy about the contract. No matter that it seemed innocuous, Sula feared being entrapped in some shady scheme that would get her in trouble.

Lord Peltrot took Sula into his private office, a very functional space with a desk of transparent material, photos and models of ships belonging to the Manado Company, and great bay windows overlooking the port. Because Peltrot spent so much time there, the air held more than a whiff of his perpetually decaying, perpetually renewing flesh. Sula stepped to the windows in a kind of reflex, as if they might bring fresh air, but they were sealed against the tropic heat. She gazed out to see the cones of volcanic islands—three, four, five—all visible on the brilliant blue of the sea. The volcanoes all had clouds obscuring their peaks, but Sula didn't know whether this was smoke from the craters or merely cloud.

"Are the volcanoes active?"

"Yes, yes, they are. Some of them, anyway. There are

more just to the east, but you can't see them from here." His tone was dismissive.

"Are there eruptions?"

"Small ones. Mahawu—that's one of the ones you can't see—blew up about twelve years ago. Some of the suburbs had to be evacuated, but only temporarily, and it's been quiet since."

"I've never been on a planet with such active geology. It takes a little getting used to."

Peltrot stepped behind his desk and gestured toward the visitor's chair. "Would you care to sit? May I offer you coffee, tea? Wine, perhaps?"

"Tea would be pleasant, thank you."

Peltrot ordered tea. Sula sat in a businesslike gray arm-chair that immediately adjusted itself to her Terran physique. Lord Peltrot sat in a larger, more plush version of the same chair.

"Lady Sula." Lord Peltrot's voice had changed to a deeper, more resonant tone. His fixed, expressionless belligerence, his perfectly round gleaming black eyes, seemed focused entirely on Sula. "I'd like to bring up the matter of the contract for use of your Fleet dockyard."

"Of course."

"I am concerned that you have not signed it. Our own lawyers and the Judge Martial have both approved the wording."

The sound of a rivet gun hammered from the boat-yard, and Sula's heart quickened as if in response. She adjusted herself in the chair and faced Peltrot squarely.

"You realize that the original agreement was signed before my appointment," she said. "And discovering such an unusual arrangement naturally raised questions in my mind."

"Questions were not raised before," Peltrot replied.

"Perhaps not, but still—"

"I should think our arrangement was perfectly clear."

Sula looked at him directly. "What was it you found out there?"

There was a moment of silence, the masklike face rigid, the black eyes staring. Behind the pale immobile lips, Sula saw mouthparts shifting, chewing the air.

"That is confidential," Peltrot said finally. "That has always been understood."

"It's clear to anyone that you've found something, presumably something valuable."

A discordant timbre entered Peltrot's voice. "I thought it had been agreed that this sort of inquiry was not the province of the Fleet."

Sula allowed impatience to show in her voice. "I don't know what you're bringing into my dockyard," she said. "It's possible you might be carrying hazardous materials, in which case—"

"There are no hazardous materials!" Peltrot's voice sounded like crashing bells. "There is no danger whatever to your station or your personnel!"

"That's as may be—"

The door opened and a dark-skinned Terran steward entered pushing a tea trolley. There was a long, ungainly silence as Sula's tea was poured, as Peltrot was given a violet-colored beverage. Sula dropped three sugars into her cup and stirred. The steward exited with his trolley, and Lord Peltrot again turned his formidable lidless gaze on Sula.

"There is no possibility of altering the arrangement," he said.

"I haven't asked for—"

"*You will have no more!*" Peltrot proclaimed. "Everything was agreed!"

The vehemence startled her. Apparently, he thought she was demanding a bribe. "I have asked for nothing—" she began.

"*The agreement must be signed!*" The Daimong voice sounded like a ship dying, bulkheads cracking, crew shrieking, atmosphere venting into space. "*There is no more room for negotiation!*"

Fury burned like a blowtorch along Sula's nerves, and she stood. "I have asked only for information!" she snapped.

But Lord Peltrot's words had gained momentum, and he talked right over her in a voice of tortured metal. The scent of his dying flesh came off him in a wave, and Sula's stomach turned. "All was decided! There were no objections! You must sign the agreement as it stands, and with no conditions!"

"*I need do nothing!*" Sula shouted into the din. Lord Peltrot fell silent, the round empty eyes like the barrels of a shotgun.

"I am not required to do anything at all," Sula said. "It is entirely up to me whether the agreement is signed or not, and right now, I am not inclined to sign it."

Lord Peltrot's words came out as a deep baritone overlaid with discordant harmonies. "It would be in your interest," he said.

"I will judge my own interest, thank you," Sula said. "I think this interview is at an end."

Vibrating with anger, Sula put on her cap and marched out. She called Macnamara with her sleeve display and had to wait outside for no more than a few seconds before the car glided to a stop in front of the building. The door rolled up, and Sula stepped inside.

"Train station," she said. And thought, *What the hell just happened?*

On the way to the station, she called Parku at the dockyard. "I need to find out everything there is to know about Lord Peltrot Convil and the Manado Company," she said.

"My lady, I've sent you everything I've discovered."

"Enlarge your inquiries. And set Koridun to work as well, and tell her to work it from the security and intelligence angle—and at this point, I'm past caring whether either of you are discreet."

There was a pause somewhat longer than that required for a signal to bounce to the ring and back. "Very good, my lady," said Parku.

Sula ended the transmission.

What was she now? Angry, baffled, and hip-deep in something she didn't understand.

The train flew upward over arches that looked as tenuous as spiders' webs as it raced into the Minahasa Highlands. The roadbed ran along the rims of volcanic craters, and Sula could look down to see blue lakes, small settlements, brilliant green rice fields, terraces, and steam rising from hot springs. Occasional whiffs of sulphur floated through the compartment as the train neared the outpourings of hot water.

The route took them curving along the Gulf of Tomini to the south, and in the distance Sula could see the receivers of the Sulawesi Rectenna Field spread like lily pads over the water, where they received microwave energy beamed down from the antimatter ring and converted to enough electricity to power the entire island. Below the surface, in the lightless shadow of the great receiver field, were the underwater command station and a hotel for underwater tourism. Sula couldn't quite imagine what attracted people to depth and darkness and pressure, especially when the bright colors of the surface beckoned everywhere she looked.

Looking south, she saw an optical illusion—one moment, the brilliant equatorial sky was unmarked, the next, the vertical black line of the elevator cables appeared as if produced by a magician from behind a celestial cape. Sula could see the cables reach up into the sky, toward the silver arc of the antimatter ring, where they disappeared into the haze. Sula tried to work out the type of refraction that had made this possible—was it "looming?"—but before she could solve the problem, the arrival at Tambu was announced.

The elevator terminus was at, or rather above, the city of Tambu, on the eastern side of Sulawesi's northern peninsula. As the train drifted into the station, Sula grinned as she saw it had been built in the Dhai-ro style, like the elevator terminus at Nairobi.

Sula acquired a Fleet car, traveled down the high

ridge above the town, and checked into the Hotel Imperial—built in the more recent, geometric Devis mode—where in the evening she would be joined by Lady Ermina Vaswati, Caro's cousin Goojie. That left the afternoon free, and Sula decided to implement her own version of Goojie's proactive policy.

The retired warrant officer who staffed the Fleet recruiting office in Tambu was jolted into terror by the sight of a celebrated war hero, the victor of Zanshaa, stalking into his office in full dress, medals gleaming, green eyes glittering with purpose. The Lai-own leaped to her feet, her feathery hair flying, and as her old reflexes took over, she snapped to attention, braced, her throat bared in submission before the sickle-shaped knife Sula wore at her belt.

"As you were," Sula said, amused. The recruiter wasn't required to brace: she'd retired from the military and technically was a civilian employee of the Fleet, and thus someone who was not obliged to offer her life to an officer at every possible opportunity.

The recruitment office was small, most of it taken up by cubicles for administering tests to aspiring recruits. The Fleet was desirable employment for the average Terran, and hundreds of thousands applied every year for the smallish number of places available.

It took all of ten minutes for Sula to ask her questions

and conclude her inspection, during which time the ex-warrant officer calmed down and, in the end, asked for a picture with Sula so that she could put it on the wall and impress the recruits. Sula obliged, trying to look martial, and then she complimented her employee on her operation and left. She proclaimed the proactive policy a success.

Afterward, she wandered around Tambu and found it a typical port town, with a population drawn from every race, world, and class in the empire. There were at least as many Naxids as humans, and again they made her nervous. Bustling commerce was everywhere, but there was nothing in the shops she couldn't find in any other major city. The equatorial heat and humidity gave her a headache, and she had Macnamara drive her back to the hotel.

Later, she was back in the car to pick up Goojie. The terminal was a vast structure built on the hill, with a swooping portico. Standing in the arrival lounge, Sula looked up through a transparent ceiling to watch the big car drop down the great cable to a lodging in its bay, then went into the arrival lounge to await processing. She had time for a cup of tea before Goojie arrived. For a moment, Goojie seemed like a strange distortion in a mirror, Sula's pale face and pale gold hair atop someone else's body, implausibly dressed in a casual tropical gown streaked artfully with several shades of pale blue, followed by two uniformed porters supervising a vast array of baggage, and a female valet with long pipestem legs and dark hair cut severely short, whose downcast eyes were focused firmly on her sleeve display, which she was jabbing with some urgency.

"Caro!" Goojie waved extravagantly and rushed on golden glittering platform shoes to clasp Sula in a warm familial embrace scented with chypre. Sula politely reciprocated the embrace, then disengaged and tugged her disarrayed undress tunic back into position.

"Caroline," she said. "I'm really not Caro anymore."

"I'll try to remember."

Sula and Goojie returned to the car, where Macnamara and the various porters eventually gave up trying to fit all Goojie's bags into the luggage compartment and had to summon a taxi to bring the bags, along with the valet, to the hotel.

"Did you really need so much luggage?" Sula asked.

"I've got to represent my family and the company in any conceivable social situation and in any possible climate."

"Ah. That's where uniforms come in handy."

Goojie eyed Sula's uniform. "That dark green color suits you well enough, but don't you think uniforms lack joy and self-expression?"

"For me," Sula said, "a uniform *is* self-expression."

"Well," said Goojie, "we'll fix *that*."

Sula considered this. The uniforms had suited her well when she was a weapon, when they had fitted her like a scabbard. But now that she was a weapon no longer, perhaps the simplicity of the uniform was no longer desirable.

"I brought a lot more clothes and other gear with me," Goojie went on, "but that's going to my office and quarters in Quito along with the rest of my servants."

Goojie, Sula decided, was surrounded by clouds: a cloud of chypre, a cloud of servants, a cloud of possessions. Sula had remained fairly cloud-free, but she'd ended up in the same place as Goojie anyway, a useless job on a dead-end world.

Except Goojie, at least, had expectations of something better.

Conversation over dinner, and on the Kan-fra aircraft the next day, was pleasant and trouble-free. Goojie talked about the teachers at her and Caro's old school—who, being much the same as teachers everywhere, seemed familiar even though Sula had never met them. Goojie chatted of former schoolmates who Sula professed not to remember, and discussed policies and personalities at the Kan-fra company.

On the flight over the Pacific, sipping tea with the

sound of atmosphere hissing along the hull, Sula found herself talking about her time at the academy, and mentioned some of her less toxic war experiences. Goojie had been untouched by the war, safe on Preowyn, though a cousin of hers had been a prisoner taken at Magaria, released when the system had been retaken. He had undergone hardship, apparently. *Whole days without bathing,* Sula assumed, *and a lousy climate, too.*

"You released him," Goojie said. "When you and the Fleet came in."

"I didn't do it personally."

"There was a lot of wartime secrecy, but I made a point of following you as much as I could. Your squadron did very well, and there you were, right out front. Everyone else in the battle seemed to take a beating."

Sula smiled and sipped her tea. This was what had so exercised the overbearing Danitz. She told Goojie of the encounter with the Democracy Club.

"So, what *was* your secret?" Goojie asked.

Sula smiled to herself. "I had the squadron fly along the convex hull of a chaotic dynamic system."

Goojie's wine glass paused halfway to her lips. "I don't know what any of that means."

"It was against orders—and worse, a *success*—and so here I am, on Earth, out of the way. It's probably my last command, at least until Supreme Commander Tork dies, and he's likely to go on forever."

"I still don't understand what you did."

"I could explain it, but why bother?"

"Tell me. I want to know more than that Danitz person." She waved at one of the aircraft's stewards. "But I want to top up my wine first. Are you sure you won't have any?"

"I'm sure," Sula said. Goojie seemed unable to understand that she didn't drink alcohol, which was understandable perhaps in anyone who knew Caro Sula.

"Oh, well," Goojie said. "More tea, then?"

An hour later, the aircraft arrowed to a water landing in Canterbury Bight, a huge wall of foam rising up to curtain the hull, pale green seawater sluicing the windows, the lap belt biting Sula's abdomen . . . and then, as the windows cleared, Sula saw the broad bulk of the Timaru volcano shouldering its way out of the waters, steam rising from a vent on its black, gleaming flank.

"Active geology," she said. "I can't seem to get away from it."

————

Titanic figures of Earth's great heroes loomed over the white marble roadway. Kong Fuzi, Shihuangdi, Elizabeth I, Rameses II, Cyrus, Augustus, Peter the Great, Ashoka,

Justinian, Josef Stalin, Louis XIV, Mao Zedong.

"All established systems that prefigured the Praxis," said their guide. "But all such Terran systems, lacking the perfect rigor of the eternal Praxis, failed over time."

Lord and Lady Macedoin, partisans of Terran history, had constructed the Arch over eight hundred years before, a great blazing white bridge that leaped over the entrance to Akaroa harbor, making whole again the great circle of the extinct crater that formed the bay. The statues, plated in gleaming copper, were sixteen times life size and stood in niches inset on the arch's façade. For the most part, they were in dynamic postures: gesturing, brandishing weapons, summoning, offering, or calling history to witness their great decisions. Their postures seemed unstable, and the guide went into detail concerning their internal structure and the ways in which they were anchored to the bridge.

"They've survived many earthquakes and the eruptions of the Timaru volcano. Twice in recent history, the roadway was buried in volcanic ash and had to be kept clean by machinery before the machinery itself was buried. Fortunately, Lord and Lady Macedoin built well."

Goojie gestured at the Akaroa crater, craggy with deep shadowed folds, the brilliant blue water far below. The resort town of Akaroa below perched on the water's rim, the inhabitants barely visible from this great height.

"There's no chance of an eruption here?"

"No. It last erupted eight million years ago and is considered extinct."

The speaker was a tiny white-haired Terran named Shirou Yoshimitsu, another colleague of Dr. Dho-ta conscripted into being a tour guide. Presumably, his multiple degrees in history and archaeology were not normally employed in guiding tourists, but nevertheless, he seemed to have all his facts in order.

"And the *other* volcano?" Goojie asked, pointing in the other direction at the great black brute rising from the ocean, the tortured island that had so dominated the horizon on their landing.

"Timaru?" Yoshimitsu clasped his tiny hands behind his back and walked to the roadway's elaborately scrolled bronze rail. "Timaru volcano is more of a problem, my lady. It's less than four hundred years old, it's already buried the old city of Timaru on the mainland, and it's in more or less continual eruption. The volcano has three craters and at least a dozen vents."

Distance hadn't made the volcano any less menacing. Steam swirled from the vent on its side. Around the island, the sea sparkled in the bright sun, but the wind seemed to have blown all the way from Antarctica, and Sula was glad for the warmth of her undress tunic, far more suitable to New Zealand's climate than that of Sulawesi. She buttoned up the collar and mashed the cap farther down on her head.

"Are we in danger?" Goojie asked.

"No, my lady. Seismologists can predict a large eruption in advance, so there would be warning."

Goojie pulled up the collar of her jacket. Yoshimitsu, wearing a light jacket over his shirt, seemed alone in being immune to the cutting wind.

Yoshimitsu looked up at the statue of Shihuangdi that loomed overhead, a bulky, broad, bearded man who glowered at the Pacific from beneath the flat, rectangular structure that crowned his stovepipe hat. "To my mind," he said, "the most interesting choices were the historical figures who were left out. Alexander the Great, one of Earth's most interesting conquerors, isn't on the memorial, because he failed to establish a theory of government that would survive his death. Presumably, conquerors like Genghis Khan and Tamerlane were ignored for similar reasons. And Adolf Hitler—he was a contemporary of Stalin and ultimately fell victim to him—established a rule based on irrational ethnic prejudices and the persecution of a religious minority. Whereas if he had persecuted *all* religions, as Stalin did, perhaps we'd be seeing his image here. . . ."

"I was under the impression that Genghis Khan formed a very efficient government," Sula said.

She and Yoshimitsu discussed this for few moments while Goojie shivered in the cold. "Why is there only one female?" she asked, completely innocent of the complex, rather appalling answer that was then revealed to her.

"Well, I'm glad we're civilized *now*," she said. "I thank the Praxis for my implant." She added, "Might we go somewhere warm?"

She was taken below the roadway to a glass-walled gallery from which the spectacular scenery could be viewed in something like warmth, and listened for a while as Sula and Yoshimitsu discussed various aspects of Terran history. Eventually, she took advantage of a silence to ask Yoshimitsu about a wedge-shaped green stone hung around his neck on a chain.

"It's a Maori adze, my lady," Yoshimitsu said. "The Maoris were the aboriginal inhabitants of the islands before the Europeans came."

"I see," Goojie asked. "But what's a European, exactly?"

After that was explained, Yoshimitsu went on. "So, initially, my ancestors ate yours—they were great warriors. But we've been getting along well for thousands of years now."

"You're a Maori?" Sula asked.

"Yes. Would you like to hear a haka?" And then, without a pause, he began a guttural chanting accompanied by a variety of postures, most of them aggressive and threatening, along with a series of grimaces. Sula wasn't quite sure how to respond. In time, he finished with a series of cries and then an outthrust tongue, then straightened from his low stance and grinned apologetically.

"Sometimes, I get a little enthusiastic," he said. "It's more impressive when there are a lot of us together—that's a chant we do at football matches to intimidate the other side."

"Well," said Goojie, "if it's football, everything is forgiven."

Yoshimitsu smiled. "Very kind of your ladyship to say so."

A discreet chime came from Sula's sleeve display, and she stepped away while Goojie and Yoshimitsu discussed football. She triggered the video feature and saw the expressionless gray features of Lord Koz Parku, her executive officer in the dockyard. His melodious voice crooned apology.

"I hope I am not interrupting anything important, my lady," Parku said.

"No, not at all."

Parku's voice shifted to a more businesslike tone. "My lady, I ran into a dead end with the Manado Company—there's only a limited amount of information available, and we already have it—so I decided to contact people who had worked with them in the past. Did you know that the Manado Company also does marine shipping on Terra?"

"Yes, I know that."

"So, I spoke with the Lord Captain of the Port of Oakland, and—"

"Where is Oakland, exactly?"

"Yerba Buena Bay, my lady. Upper California District, North America."

"Very good. Go on."

"Now, Lord Captain of the Port is a paramilitary office—they're like the port's police. They deal with search and rescue, criminal matters, and security."

"I understand."

"And the Lord Harbormaster is a civilian official, a political appointee of the Governor of Upper California, and handles everything else in the port—tariffs, berthing, warehousing, environmental issues, and so forth."

"Very good."

"Now, the Lord Captain has heard quite a few complaints about the Manado Company from other shippers. Some have complained that the Manado ships get priority in loading and unloading. Everything is expedited for them in ways that it isn't for other companies. And Manado ships always seem to get choice berthing."

Sula laughed. "Like in a Fleet dockyard?"

An ironic buzz tinged Parku's words. "Yes. Yes, indeed."

"But none of that is in the Lord Captain's purview, yes?"

"Correct, my lady. It's the Lord Harbormaster or his assistants who make those decisions."

"It sounds as if the Manado Company has a very special arrangement with the Lord Harbormaster."

"Very likely." That ironic buzz was still present. "Now, there *have* been some criminal complaints."

"Yes?"

A tone of eagerness entered Parku's voice. "There was one ship that had its berthing assignment taken away in favor of a Manado ship. The captain claimed that she hadn't understood the garbled radio order, steered her ship into the berth anyway, and then claimed engine failure prevented her leaving. She prolonged her engine failure until her ship was unloaded and had taken on her new cargo."

"Very clever."

"Well, she paid for it. Beaten within an inch of her life by a group of thugs, and ended up spending a few weeks in the hospital."

"Any indictments?"

A chime of negation. "No, the attackers were never

identified, and no connection with the Manado Company ever surfaced. And the Lord Captain said there were other violent incidents of a similar nature from people who 'crossed Manado's hawse,' as he put it. The Lord Captain is itching to bring a prosecution, but he simply has no evidence."

Sula considered the news for a moment. "Lord Peltrot acted as if he has a habit of getting what he wants."

The melodious voice turned solemn. "The Manado Company doesn't shy at violence, my lady. Perhaps I should have Lieutenant-Captain Koridun contact you regarding your safety?"

Sula smiled. "I hardly think the Manado Company is likely to assault a Fleet captain. It would cause them too much trouble. There would be an investigation they couldn't control."

"But still—"

"Besides," Sula added, "I travel with a pair of very accomplished killers." *And,* she thought, *I'm not so bad at that sort of thing myself.*

"Very good, my lady," said Parku. Then, after a short pause: "One rather minor issue—I received a notice from the Disaster Relief Agency that the Karangetang volcano may be on the verge of erupting."

Sula frowned. "How does that concern the dockyard?"

"Karangetang is on Api Siau Island, just north of Manado. A large eruption might endanger the Tambu elevator or its facility."

Amusement twitched the corners of Sula's eyes. "We can't escape Manado, can we?"

"No, my lady."

"Very well. Keep me informed."

"Very good, my lady."

Sula and Goojie left Yoshimitsu at the Arch, and Spence drove them back to Otautahi on the other side of the Banks peninsula.

"The miniature warrior!" Goojie cried. "What a terror!"

"I can see where it might be intimidating with a lot of people chanting at once," Sula said. "But Mister Yoshimitsu—"

"Whose ancestors ate our ancestors!"

Sula sighed. "Ah, well. We have better weapons now than chants."

"And better food to eat."

Sula turned to Goojie. "What shall we do tomorrow? The west coast is supposed to be spectacular; we can take a train . . ."

"No no no. We're going to do something *I* want to do."

Sula looked at her in surprise. "It was you who wanted to go to the Arch."

"We're going to a spa in the morning, then shopping

in the afternoon. But I've got a dinner with the local Kan-fra people tonight; you're on your own."

"I—"

"It's your vacation! Pamper yourself!"

Sula sighed. She might as well.

Who was Sula now? Cousin Goojie's comic sidekick, apparently.

Sula was reluctant to credit Parku's warning about the danger from Manado, but then she remembered Lord Peltrot's ranting, and she decided that she hadn't gone on vacation to get beaten up by thugs. That night, she told Spence and Macnamara that there had been a warning, and that they should be on alert and carry sidearms. And that she'd carry a sidearm herself.

Not that she spent much of the next day in uniform. In the morning, Goojie brought her to a spa on the Banks peninsula just outside Otautahi, and while Cree musicians played soothing music in the background, there were a steam bath, massage, facial, manicure and pedicure, and she had her hair styled while a cosmetician painted a new face over her old one. She looked at the result in the mirror and blinked; the image showed a new person who looked just enough like the old Sula to seem uncanny. The cosmetician had darkened her pale complexion and created a kind of smoky effect in the eye sockets that made her eyes blaze like green fire out of some exotic extraplanetary twilight. She turned at Goojie and seemed to be looking into another mirror.

"They made me look like you!" she said.

Goojie smiled. "We're twins now."

Spence, uniformed and with her pistol, hovered in the waiting room, to the apparent distress of the Torminel manager, who didn't want such a lower-class servant in her establishment. Sula put on her captain voice and told her to lump it, and she did.

Macnamara stayed with the car to make sure someone didn't put a bomb in it. Sula thought that was a bit extreme, but at least that meant there weren't *two* guards standing around to torment the manager.

Leaving the spa, Sula noticed that her hair bounced more than it usually did.

From the spa, they went to an arcade filled with boutiques. The shop assistants clustered around them, polite and attentive and as beautifully painted and arrayed as dolls. Perfumes floated gently in the air. Dresses, gowns, sheaths, jackets, skirts, and pantaloons blossomed around them like exotic flowers. Goojie selected treasures for herself and for Sula, pushed Sula into the dressing rooms, and critiqued the result. She made Sula buy a jacket, a kurti-and-skirt combination, and a floaty gown in shades of green, similar to the blue one Goojie had worn at their first meeting.

"And is that the best underwear you've got?" Goojie asked.

Sula considered the question cautiously. "Possibly," she said.

So, then it was off to a lingerie shop, and then another stop for shoes, and then another place for jewelry, where Sula was urged to indulge in a ridiculously expensive pair of silver bracelets inset with black and red coral.

"Stop bullying me," she said.

"It's for your own good."

"Where would I wear them?"

"You could wear them tonight. At dinner and afterward."

Afterward? Sula thought, and then decided not to buy the bracelets. Goojie, having accomplished most of her objectives, let the bracelets go with a sigh. "You can come back tomorrow if you change your mind."

Sula changed to the green gown at the hotel, then Goojie carried Sula off to the C____ C____ restaurant, the name of which was inscribed above the door in old Terran script. Sula asked the Lai-own hostess what the letter stood for.

"Christchurch," she said. "It's the old name for Otau-tahi."

"Christchurch," Sula said. "Two words you can't use any more."

"Why is that?" Goojie wanted to know.

Sula explained as the hostess showed them to their table in the Terran section. Macnamara was stationed in the lounge, which had a view of the dining room, and this time, Spence stayed with the car—bombs were more her specialty, anyway.

The transparent walls of the dining room overlooked Diamond Harbour, with the lights of the ships shining like rubies and emeralds against the darkness of the bay, and the craggy peaks of the Banks Peninsula still aglow with the light of the setting sun. Wearing a new face, her body oiled and relaxed and scented, a silken gown float-ing around her, Sula felt a strange world of possibility shivering open like a pair of trembling wings. It was, she thought, a world where she was no longer at war, where she could settle into the comforts of peace and pleasure.

A world she had never known.

Goojie ordered cocktails for the both of them but was disappointed when Sula ordered soft cider instead.

"You're on vacation!"

"I still don't drink."

"Everyone's looking at us."

Sula looked at her gown to make sure something hadn't spilled on it.

"We look like twin sisters, that's why," Goojie said. "Gorgeous twin sisters. And people are wondering if a couple of gentlemen are going to join us."

"They'll be disappointed," Sula said, and then looked at Goojie with a suspicious eye. "Unless you arranged that, too?"

"No, but there are some single men here who look as if they might want to meet us. And I've got a list of clubs we can visit later, and we're bound to meet people there."

Sula nodded in the direction of Macnamara, who was visible thirty paces away, drinking fruit juice in the lounge. "Can we bring our guards?"

Goojie laughed. The idea that they might be attacked had amused her all day.

"He should frisk anyone who wants to dance with us," she said.

"That'll make us popular."

Cree music drifted through the air. The appetizers arrived on a cloud of basil and mint. Goojie ordered a chilled bottle of wine.

"I won't help you drink it," Sula warned.

"I'll order a demi, then."

They laughed and chatted through the meal, as easy as if they were actual sisters. Sula, for whom rapport hardly ever came easily, wondered at the effortlessness of it all. Perhaps she had made a friend.

Goojie poured herself a glass of wine, then paused.

"Does it bother you that I drink?" she asked.

Sula was surprised "No. Why do you ask?"

"I mean, I don't *have* to drink," Goojie said. "If it bothers you—if you have a hard time *not* drinking—I'm perfectly happy not drinking myself."

Sula shrugged. "No," she said. "It's fine."

"So, why don't you drink? You weren't—addicted?—or anything?"

"I genuinely don't care for it. And also there were some people in my life who drank too much, and they wrecked their hopes and became a danger to everyone around them."

And so I killed them, she thought, and suppressed a shudder.

And then, in a moment of awareness that fell on her like a great thundering waterfall, she realized why she had so successfully bonded with Goojie. She was reenacting her life with Caro Sula, who had pretended to be her sister, who had bought her things, who had swept Gredel along on her sad and aimless life, from spas and boutiques to restaurants and bars and clubs, careening from one bottle to the next, one injection of endorphin analogue to another. . . . Instead of proving an opening into a new life, Goojie was an excuse for Sula to fall back into an old pattern, one that felt too much like home. One that had led to disaster.

The revelation stunned her for a moment. "What's wrong?" Goojie asked.

"I—" She stared, rubbing the pad of scar tissue on her right thumb. "Nothing. Nothing's wrong."

"You look terrible. What—"

The insight had staggered Sula, and Goojie's interruption had sidetracked her mind, and so she almost missed the Naxid. Naxids were out of place in the Terran dining room, not because there was any formal segregation but because humans sat in chairs and Naxids reclined their centauroid bodies on little divans set around low tables. All the species under the Praxis required different conditions: no one wanted to be around Daimong because of the smell; the Lai-own needed a chair that cradled their keel-like breastbones; the diet of the Torminel made other species uneasy; and the Cree liked to congregate in large, noisy groups. So, in large, polished restaurants, species were seated in separate dining rooms.

The interloper scrambled into the room with the scurrying gait of the Naxids, a gray overcoat draped loosely over his quadruped frame, and his flat head swung left and right as he peered at the diners. The Naxid had come in through the back of the building, and Macnamara wouldn't have seen him. Sula's mind teetered for a moment at the sight, caught between the Naxid and Goojie and the impact of her own revelation, and then alarms began to clatter up her nerves. But by then it was too late, and the Naxid had produced a pistol . . .

After which, finger poised on the trigger, the Naxid hesitated.

Because he had two targets. Two blond Terran females with near-identical faces, flowing gowns and flowing pale hair and green eyes, and neither was in the viridian uniform that would have provided a clear identification; so it took him a second or so to reach the obvious conclusion, which was to *kill them both.* . . .

Sula kicked the table at him just as the pistol fired. The table struck the Naxid above his forelegs and threw off the second shot; and before he could line up for the third, Sula had thrown Goojie's wine bottle at his head. There was no brain in the Naxid's skull to concuss—the Naxid head was a sensory platform, and the brain safely stored in the torso—but still the bottle scrambled the assassin's perceptions long enough for Sula to launch herself from her chair.

The instructors at the Fleet's personal combat course had emphatically advised against jumping on an enemy's gun, but in this case there was little choice—Sula had to get control of the weapon before the assassin could get off another shot. And so she grabbed the Naxid's dry, scaly forearm with both hands, yanked the arm away from the body, and threw her shoulder into the enemy, low into the centaur's upper body.

Despite his four legs, the Naxid was off-balance, and he and Sula crashed to the ground with Sula on top of the gun, trying desperately to point it anywhere but at herself. The Naxid's four booted feet flailed, kicked the table, sent glasses and dinnerware clattering to the ground. There were screams. Diners jumped and scattered.

The gun went off with a deafening crash and Sula felt hot gasses flame against her cheek. The sound so jolted her nerves that she almost lost her grip on the enemy, but the Naxid wasn't fast enough at snatching his arm away, and Sula bore down with all her weight and got hold of the gun itself—hot metal scorched her fingers—and she fought to bend the wrist back, back so the Naxid would face his own weapon... and then she saw the Naxid's other arm had yanked a big knife out of his overcoat, and that it was poised to stab her. Frantically, she kicked at the Naxid, felt pain as her toes jammed into the enemy torso.

And then Macnamara was standing over them, his own pistol out. A star of the Fleet combat course, he put four shots into the Naxid, hitting brain, heart, lungs, and brain again, very professionally placing each shot so there was no danger to Sula.

Sula got the Naxid's gun out of his limp, scaled fingers and hurled it into a corner. Then she scrambled to hands and knees and groped her way to where Goojie lay dying on the wooden floor, her blue gown turning brilliant crimson with arterial blood. There was wild desperation in the jade eyes, and her bloody hands made frantic gestures in the air. Breath panted past the painted lips. Sula reached for a slightly soiled linen napkin lying next to Goojie's overturned chair and stuffed the napkin into the wound. It turned red almost at once.

"Doctor!" Sula shouted. "Ambulance!" Hoping to restore some sense of order to a room that was now pandemonium.

She applied as much pressure as possible to the napkin and stroked Goojie's head with the other hand. Goojie's hands clutched at her. The air smelled of chypre and blood.

"The ambulance is on its way," she told Goojie. "The ambulance is on its way. Only a few minutes out."

The desperation in the green eyes grew more frantic, the gestures more frenetic. Goojie's breath heaved. The napkin soaked up more red. Goojie's heels drummed the floor. The hands grabbed Sula's arms, her hair, her face. Sula remembered bending over Caro's body like this, except that she had wanted Caro to die, and now she wanted Goojie to live.

There was a clattering and Sula was aware of Spence dashing in, her own pistol ready. Sula remained focused on the victim, and Spence knelt down to join her, trying to restrain the flailing limbs. Goojie kept fighting, her eyes ever more desperate until they flattened and the color faded, until the last heaving spasms shivered through her. The clutching hands fell away.

People did not, in Sula's experience, die as easily and cleanly as in a video drama.

Sula looked into the dead face and saw Caro Sula looking back at her. Through her shock, she heard the sound of weeping and looked up to see some of the diners standing in a half-circle around the body, as helpless as Sula to alter the presence of mortality once it had entered in the room.

Sula rose tottering on her new heels, cleared a nearby table, and swept off the tablecloth to put it over Caro's blank, bloody face. She found a chair and sat in it and stared out the window at the glittering harbor, the dark volcanic peaks of the Banks peninsula looming above the water. Her heartbeat surged, faded, surged again. She could feel blood drying on her face. The emotions that had burned through her in the last few minutes seemed to have settled down into something like disgust.

Macnamara was still standing guard in the center of the room, pistol in hand. The air tasted of propellant and the coppery scent of blood.

Burly uniformed Torminel marched in carrying a folded-up stretcher, and the tablecloth was removed so that they could confirm the death. Sula didn't want to look, and didn't. From Goojie, the Torminel went to the assassin, confirmed his death as well, and then left the bodies for the police. One came up to Sula and asked if she was injured.

"I am unharmed," she said with finality, and the Torminel retreated to the lounge, from which he kept a wary eye on her.

The first police arrived in blue uniforms and black leather shakoes, took one look at the place, and called for backup. More police arrived in even grander uniforms, all careful not to step in the blood with their shiny shoes. The grandest of them, a chief inspector, was a Daimong who added the fetor of his dying flesh to the room. He told Sula that their conversation would be recorded, and asked Sula for her name.

"Captain the Lady Sula," she said.

The Torminel's fixed face could not alter, but there was something in his posture that shifted to an attitude of greater attention. "You are *the* Lady Sula?" he inquired.

"There's only one Lady Sula, so far as I know."

Sula rose and managed to stand steadily on her heels. The chief inspector straightened, looking at her with black, round eyes. "I would like to make a statement," she said. "I do not know the assassin, but I'm reasonably certain he was hired by Lord Peltrot Convil of the Manado Company, based in Manado, Sulawesi. I am involved in a contract dispute with him in my capacity as commander of the Fleet dockyard. The assassin entered the room from *there.*" She pointed. "He was intending to kill me but instead shot my cousin, Lady Ermina Vaswani, by mistake. I then tried to disarm the attacker, and we both ended up on the ground until the Naxid was shot and killed by my guard, Constable First Class Gavin Macnamara."

The inspector made a chiming sound, then spoke. "Very . . . comprehensive, my lady."

Sula was aware of a fierce harshness inflecting her words, but she couldn't seem to curb her tone. "I would now like to go to my hotel and bathe. I will report to you in the morning to make a further statement and answer any questions."

The chief inspector apparently contemplated his authority and decided it did not quite extend to holding a hero of the empire. "Your guard will have to surrender his weapon," he said.

Macnamara put his pistol on a table, Sula gave the

name of her hotel to the chief inspector, and she was asked to sign a printout of her statement. She signed the single title Sula and added the print of her left, undamaged, thumb. Then Macnamara and Spence hustled her out of the restaurant and to the car. She was put in the back, and then the two servants jumped into the front and sped away. Spence, in the passenger seat, dropped the window to the passenger compartment and turned to look at Sula.

"Are you all right, my lady?"

Sula sighed and closed her eyes. Splashes of scarlet pulsed on the back of her eyelids. "I suppose I must be," she said.

Disgust filled her senses like the reek of blood. Disgust at the tawdriness of the world, at the sordid hopelessness of the violence, at her own carelessness, at Goojie's stupidity in dying for nothing.

In her hotel suite, she threw her new clothes in the trash and stepped into the shower. She cleaned off the blood and let water rinse the taste of propellant from her mouth. She washed off the new face the cosmetician had applied, then scrubbed herself with sandalwood-scented soap until she smelled like a forest grove. Then she wrapped herself in a towel, scrubbed mist off the mirror, and looked at the pale, green-eyed figure in the glass, the lank, wet hair framing her face. She raised her hand, forefinger pointed like a pistol, and aimed at her own image. She made a puffing pistol noise with her lips.

That's what this is about, she thought. *And this is who I am.*

"Lady Sula," said Lieutenant-Captain Koridun, "I must insist on sending my constables to guard you. And I'll come myself to supervise."

Her image, gray and sable, shone from the chameleon-weave fabric of Sula's sleeve display. Behind the security officer was her workplace, with the badge of the Fleet constabulary prominent on the wall. Koridun the Correct, fur glossy and well tended, alert to the possibility of notice and advance.

"Send the constables, by all means," Sula told her. "But I don't know that this matter will require your presence."

"There is also the matter of the investigation—"

"I'm afraid the police will insist on doing the investigation themselves."

Agitated, Koridun spat the words out through her fangs. "My lady, I am trained in investigative techniques, and—"

"Your dedication is commendable, Lady Tari," Sula said. "But I need you to employ your investigative techniques in another matter—I want you to trace Lady Ermina Vaswani's movements on the ring. It occurs to me that I have no idea whether she was actually on the *Benin* or not, or on the ring, or for that matter, whether she was the person she claimed to be."

Sula didn't have these doubts herself; she simply didn't want Koridun coming down to Terra. It would be awkward to have a constabulary officer present when Sula ordered someone murdered.

"As for the constables," Sula said, "equip them with pistols, stun batons, and armor. Have them bring civilian clothes in case these prove necessary, and bring a couple machine pistols as well." She was tempted to add *and grenades* but decided against it. "Some," she said, "will need experience in driving motor vehicles."

"Very good, my lady. But—"

"I'm afraid I have an appointment at police headquarters," Sula said. "Let me know if there's progress."

She ended the transmission and leaned back on the seat of her car. Otautahi passed by the windows in bland procession, the buildings raised, wrecked by earthquake, then raised again, the sequence repeated over and over until the structures were as bland and utilitarian as possible, built in the foreknowledge of the quake that would damage them beyond repair and that anything beyond simple functionality was pointless. Who would craft something beautiful, knowing that it would be destroyed?

The car rocked over a pothole, throwing Sula forward, then back. A lance of pain impaled her head. She had slept very little, and all night, the fight in the restaurant had kept replaying itself in her mind. Whenever sleep caught her, she jolted awake with Caro's dead eyes staring at her from out of the darkness.

Police headquarters was another undistinguished building, marked only by an allegorical statue of the Great Master Presenting Perfect Justice to the People. She passed through the steel, fortresslike doors in her full dress uniform, ceremonial knife clanking at her waist, medals ranked on her chest, sidearm in its holster.

The Torminel chief inspector was, she gathered, of insufficient rank to take her statement, and she was shown into the magnificently equipped office of Lady Gudrun Bjorge, the Commissioner of Police for New Zealand and the Chatham Isles. She was a burly woman with graying blond hair and wore a magnificent uniform of midnight blue fabric, with vermilion collar, cuffs, and brocade. Her rows of medals dwarfed Sula's, and there was a polished piece of green stone, cut in a spiral design, pinned to her tunic. Her office was paneled in great shining bronze sheets, and there was a smaller version of the Great Master and his Perfect Justice standing behind her desk. Probably, the commissioner had paid for all that herself:

high-ranking officials competed in expensive and elegant decor.

"Lady Sula," she said. "I am honored by your presence."

Sula began to suspect from this opening that the interrogation would go well.

"Thank you, Lady Commissioner," she said. If she'd been in a better mood, she might have said that the honor was all hers, but she was too wracked by the previous few hours to care much about the forms.

"Please take a chair. Would you like coffee or a beverage?"

"I'd prefer tea, if that's possible."

Lady Gudrun sat behind her gleaming bronze desk and summoned tea. "I'd like to have someone here to make an official record," she said. "Is that acceptable to you?"

"Certainly."

Tea and the recorder came in at the same time, the latter a meek Lai-own in a sky-blue uniform. The recorder sat in a chair to the side and deployed his instruments. A servant put a large silver carafe of coffee on the desk for the commissioner and poured tea for Sula. The cups were beautiful translucent hard-paste porcelain, leaf-thin, with a heraldic blazon, presumably that of the commissioner herself.

"First," Lady Gudrun said, "the killer has been identi-fied. He was Naktar Fargu, age thirty-one, a professional criminal who has spent half his adult life in labor camps. It's not known whether he was an actual member of one of our organized crime families or not—here on Terra, they're called *mafia*."

"On Zanshaa, they're *handmen*," Sula said.

"I know." The commissioner gave her an austere look. "As I was saying, it's not clear whether Fargu was a mem-ber of the mafia or simply associated with mafia mem-bers. He's not been linked with murder before, but that doesn't mean he hasn't killed people, just that he wasn't caught. And as for his weapon, it was reported stolen sixty-three years ago and has been involved in crimes all around the world in the years since."

"That speaks to his criminal connections," Sula said. She sipped her tea, added more sugar, sipped again.

The commissioner nodded. "His last residence was Sydney, and he arrived in Otautahi two days ago on a ground-effects liner."

"Fast worker, then." Sula tried to recall if she'd noticed any Naxids hanging around during her day of shopping, stalking her, but couldn't recall any—and her senses had been sharpened by months of fighting the Naxids in an urban environment. She'd have to ask Macnamara and Spence.

"Is Sydney a port?" Sula asked.

"Yes." Lady Gudrun tilted her head. "Why does that matter?"

"It might be interesting to discover if the Manado Company has offices there."

"I'll make a point of finding out." She sipped coffee and gave a little frown. "Last night, you made an accusation regarding this Manado Company. I would like some substantiation of that allegation, if you will."

Sula gave the information she possessed. As she spoke, she sensed that her report was less than convincing—she didn't know why Lord Peltrot wanted the berth in the Fleet yard; what the *Manado* had found, or was seeking, in the Kuiper Belt; or why Lord Peltrot would be willing to take such a risky step as the assassination of a very public figure.

"My own investigation has shown that the Manado Company uses violence to achieve their ends," she concluded. "You might want to have someone talk to the Lord Captain of the Port in Oakland—or indeed the lord captains of any port in which the Manado Company maintains an office."

"That shall certainly be done." The commissioner looked down at her desk and frowned. "It might be said that the fact of the attacker's being a Naxid is significant. You killed a great many Naxids during the war. Could this have been a simple act of vengeance by Fargu on behalf of the lost Naxid cause?"

"If he were acting alone, how did he track me so well? He arrived in New Zealand the same day I did."

"I didn't say *alone*. I said an act of vengeance—there could be others involved."

"I haven't seen any Naxids keeping me under observation."

"I ask because Fargu's elder sister was in the Fleet and was reported killed at Antopone."

Sula gestured with her cup. "I didn't kill her. I wasn't present at that battle."

"Other loyalist commanders aren't on Terra, within range of Fargu's vengeance." The commissioner let this hang in the air for moment, then sighed. "Well. It's a theory we'll have to investigate."

"*You* will," Sula said. "I won't."

Lady Gudrun paused for a moment, her lips pursing in and out in time with her thoughts, and then she went on to another item in her mental checklist.

"Your cousin, Lady Ermina," she said. "How well did you know her?"

"We were friends in childhood. This was the first I'd seen her in many years."

"Do you think it's possible that the killer intended to kill Lady Ermina rather than you?"

Sula repressed a snarl. "I suppose that's another theory you'll have to investigate," she said.

Any theory, she thought, that avoided the possibility that the killer had been hired by the Manado Company, because that made the investigation too complicated and too unlikely to get results. Professional killers who died on the job were unlikely to give up answers but were also unlikely to resist a simplistic theory being attached to them.

Lady Gudrun looked up. "I want to give you my personal guarantee that anyone involved with Lady Ermina's death will find justice."

"I'm assured beyond measure," Sula said. "And by the way, can Constable/First Macnamara get his sidearm back?"

"I understand that tests have been completed," said Lady Gudrun. "I'll have it delivered to the reception desk by the main doors." She turned to the recorder. "I believe that completes my questions," she said.

Sula put down her tea and rose from her seat. "Thank you," she said.

The commissioner's medals jangled as she rose. "*Haere ra,*" she said.

"I'm sorry?"

"I wished you farewell in Maori," she said.

Sula noted again the spiral green stone, the same color

as Yoshimitsu's adze, pinned to the commissioner's tunic.

"You are Maori?" she asked.

"Yes," said Lady Gudrun Bjorge. "In fact, I'm Ariki Tauoroa of the Ngai Tahu—chief of a large tribe."

Sula frowned. "Isn't it contrary to the Praxis to have those sorts of quasi-governmental institutions?"

Lady Gudrun spread her big hands. "We are a long way from Zanshaa, Lady Sula."

"Indeed we are," said Sula.

On her way out, she retrieved Macnamara's pistol and handed it to him once she was safely in the car. As Spence pulled the car onto the road, Sula's sleeve display gave a discreet chime, and Sula answered to see the unlined face, goatee, and perfect black hair of Lord Moncrieff Ngeni.

"Lord Governor," she said.

"I wanted to contact you in view of the incident yesterday," said Lord Moncrieff. "I'm shocked that this occurred during your stay here, and I wanted to offer you my condolences on the death of Lady Ermina."

"Thank you, Lord Moncrieff. I very much appreciate your taking the time to contact me yourself."

There was a moment's silence as the signal bounced up to the ring, then down to Constantinople, and then Lord Moncrieff replied. "I have already been in touch with the local authorities to let them know I'll be taking a personal interest. I hope they're treating you with every consideration."

Sula considered mentioning the commissioner's preference for simplistic solutions, but decided that such a complaint was both premature and, likely, futile. "Lady Commissioner Bjorge gave me her personal guarantee that those responsible would be found."

There was a moment of silence, and then a look of bewilderment settled onto Lord Moncrieff's face. "Found? I thought you had dealt with the killer yourself, Lady Sula."

"Lord Governor, he is unlikely to have acted alone."

"Ah. I see." His look darkened. "Fanatics of some sort, no doubt. This planet breeds fanatics faster than it breeds ants."

Sula had only a slight idea of what ants might be but agreed anyway. "Lord Governor," she said, "I wonder if you could possibly find some information for me."

"Of course, Lady Sula. If I can."

"I'm interested in discovering the ownership of the Manado Company, a shipping company based in Manado, Sulawesi."

There was a moment's confusion as Lord Moncrieff fumbled with his hand comm. "Just a moment, Lady Sula, while I set this device to record. Will you repeat that, please?"

Sula repeated the information, then added, "It's a privately held company, so the information isn't public, but I know records must be held somewhere on Terra. I know nothing about forming companies myself, so I don't know which agencies would have the information."

There was an out-of-focus image as Lord Moncrieff peered at his hand comm from close range to make certain he'd recorded properly. "I can locate that for you, my lady," he said finally. "May I ask why?"

"The chairman of the Manado Company threatened me four days ago, and yesterday, someone tried to kill me. I suspect the two facts are related."

"By the All!" Lord Moncrieff was shocked. "I shall certainly bring you that information!"

"The Manado Company wants to base their warship in the Fleet dockyards," Sula added. "I was inclined to turn them down, but—"

"A warship! A privately held warship!" Lord Moncrieff stared. "How can such a thing exist?"

Sula explained how the *Bombardment of Utgu* had been turned into a privately owned ship that ventured into the Kuiper Belt. "It's my understanding that no weaponry was ever installed. But now I'm determined to inspect that ship as soon as it can be arranged."

"They may be fanatics!" Lord Moncrieff was thoroughly alarmed. "With a warship they could threaten the entire planet!"

Sula saw no reason to mollify the lord governor's anxiety. "They're up to something, my lord. That contract dates from before my time, but perhaps it's time to revisit it."

"Indeed." Lord Moncrieff chewed his upper lip. "Does the Lady Commissioner have this information?"

"Yes," Sula said. "But of course she has to be scrupulous and investigate all possible alternatives, such as the killer acting alone."

"Hardly likely!" Scornfully. "I shall certainly speak with the Lady Commissioner about this!"

Sula smiled. "I shall be most grateful, Lord Moncrieff."

Well, she thought. *That worked out well.*

Sometimes, people of limited intelligence could be very useful.

———

Between her military rank and her status as a Peer, Sula had no problem purchasing four pistols and a shotgun, all of them quite beautiful, with grips of rare woods and barrels engraved with arabesque designs. While the Shaa conquerors hadn't wanted firearms widely available to ordinary people, they wanted their Peer proxies to be able to participate fully both in the suppression of rebellion and in the usual aristocratic blood sports, and so firearms were simply taxed to the point where most people couldn't afford them. There was of course a subculture of people who built their own, but these were regularly culled and the unlucky killed publicly, in appalling ways, as a deterrent to others.

However beautiful her weapons, Sula and her party were now well armed enough to begin an insurrection.

Before her purchase was complete, Sula received a message from the morgue informing her that Goojie's autopsy had been completed, and that the body was being released to her. The rest of the day was spent dealing with arranging for the cremation and for Goojie's ashes to be sent to her family on Chijimo. Sula would have to send them a personal message, but she put that job off till later. While she was engaged with the morgue and its paperwork and the undertaker with even more paperwork, her display buzzed with one message after another: the commissioner, presumably still riding the rocket the Lord Governor had ignited under her, and who assured Sula that she was taking the Manado accusation seriously; Parku offering condolences; Koridun making another play to take personal command of Sula's guards; Ratnasari sending sympathy from Constantinople... even Adele Souka, Jack Danitz, and other members of the Democracy Club expressing their condolences, though these last didn't have her direct address but sent their messages courtesy of her office in the Fleet dockyard. There were also a great many requests from journalists for statements or interviews—the story was already being widely reported, and the attempted assassination of a decorated hero of the Naxid War was a story that carried its own sensationalism with it. As a result of the story, sympathy now flooded in from thousands of perfect strangers.

The journalists were persistent enough that Sula decided they had to be dealt with, and she and Parku and Lady Gudrun's office worked out a statement to be released through Sula's office—it was brief, with Goojie's biography, another of the killer, and an expression of Sula's confidence that justice would prevail. It also declined all interview requests.

"And by the way," Parku said finally. "It looks as if Karangetang is going to blow. I can start to make preparations if you're too busy."

It took a moment for Sula to remember that Karangetang was the island volcano just north of Manado. "Is there established procedure for an eruption this close to the skyhook?" she asked.

"Yes. This sort of thing has happened before. Normally, we send a team to the surface to see to the physical safety of the facility. The cars are sent up to the ring to be out of danger, and engineers stand ready to release the cables from their moorings if their integrity is ever compromised."

"Right. For now, err on the side of excess. Have at least twice as many crew standing by as the plan calls for."

"Very good, my lady."

The day was long, and late that evening, Sula was back in her hotel, eating a room service bowl of clear, fragrant broth with little zieg-filled dumplings and scallions, when she received the documents from the Lord Governor's office. She linked her sleeve display to the video in the room and paged through the available information on the Manado Company. Whomever Lord Moncrieff had assigned to the duty had done a very thorough job.

The Manado Company had been formed a year or so before the war, by one Aram, Lord Tacorian in partnership with a Madeleine Patel. Lord Tacorian ran a small shipping company with business entirely in the Sol system, and Patel was one of his captains. Just before the Naxid War broke out, the company acquired an investor in the form of Lord Mogna, a wealthy Daimong Peer in Zanshaa High City who happened to be patron to the Tacorian clan. The Manado Company began acquiring ships, a practice that continued during the war when various shipping lines were going under due to war losses.

The company also acquired an ocean-shipping firm on Terra and with it Lord Peltrot Convil, who had successfully managed the Terran firm and who was now put in charge of the entire Manado Company. Around the same time, Lord Mogna probably made some backdoor arrangements for the *Bombardment of Utgu* to be purchased.

To Sula it seemed clear enough. Captain Patel had found something in the Kuiper Belt, and she and Tacorian had found a company to exploit it. Tacorian had brought in funding via his patron in the capital, bought the ships suitable for harnessing the discovery, and then hired an experienced hand capable of managing a larger company.

More names were added to the list of owners, and Sula recognized most of them as important members of the Convocation, those in a position to vote the Manado Company rights to whatever it was they had discovered. And then, down at the bottom of the list, Sula encountered the final name.

Caroline, Lady Sula.

"Ah. Hah." She stared at the name for a long while, and then at the figures that followed the name. She computed the numbers in her head to discover that she owned something like four percent of the Manado Company, and until that moment, she hadn't even known it.

She wondered if Lord Peltrot Convil had bribed her, then forgotten to tell her what he'd done.

And then, in a rush of amazed wonder so sudden it left her breathless, Sula realized what was happening. *I'm being set up.*

Sula's first impulse was to call Lady Gudrun and tell the commissioner what she'd discovered, and then she realized that she couldn't tell anyone at all, because it would look more like a confession than a clue. It would look as if she were trying to wriggle out of a corruption charge by claiming that she hadn't known the bribe existed in the first place.

How long before Lady Gudrun finds this out?

Then she looked at the date of the document and felt another surge of astonishment. The shares had been assigned to her *weeks* ago. While she was still in the dockyards on the ring, well before she'd seen the *Manado* or heard of the Manado Company. Long before she'd had any kind of conflict with the company, long before she'd ever heard of Lord Peltrot Convil.

So, whoever was setting her up hadn't intended a *conflict* with the Manado Company, had in fact wished to make it look like Sula was doing the Manado Company all manner of illicit favors.

What other *favors am I supposed to have done?* It was only because of a dispute with the Manado Company that she'd investigated and found this surprising addition to her portfolio. She wondered how many other bribes had come her way without her knowing anything about them.

And if they had, where *were* they?

A spinning whirlpool of speculation filled Sula's head, a maelstrom in which the very few facts she knew tried desperately to stay afloat. She wondered if there were a bank or brokerage account with her name on it, and if there were, how it could be found. And she supposed that Lady Gudrun and the police could find the information a lot more easily than she could.

And if *she* were her unknown enemy, she'd be quietly tipping off the police right now about the existence of those funds.

She pushed away her dumpling soup and rose from the table to pace back and forth between the two main rooms of her suite. Sula knew her time was running out: soon it would look very much as if the assassin had been sent by some character she was supposed to have been in business with, and that would be the end of that. She'd be disgraced and probably executed, just as the late Lord and Lady Sula had been.

Sula needed to know who might have been involved in

payments, and how many payments there were, and how they'd been made without her knowledge, and where they were. She needed a lot of information, but she had no investigative authority and no way of prying open the records of banks or brokerages or other financial institutions.

If only she'd toured banks, she thought, instead of Terra's monuments.

The thought called to mind her adventures in Constantinople with Ratnasari, and the tedious meeting of the Democracy Club, who had bored her senseless but then sent her condolences on Goojie's death. She remembered Jack Danitz, who claimed to have researched her, and Adele Souka, the red-haired woman who had claimed to have met her... and then she realized, *It wasn't me she met.*

It had been someone who *looked* like Sula. Someone who looked enough like her to confuse an assassin and apparently Souka as well.

Goojie! The wave of surprise struck Sula with an almost-physical impact, but on further reflection, it was clear that Goojie had to be involved somehow. She'd been posing as Sula, negotiating with people like Lord Peltrot and accepting bribes to discredit her.

It seemed an elaborate plot, and an expensive one, for no apparent return; and then Sula began to wonder which of her relatives would inherit the Sula title if she died. She'd assumed all along that the title would become extinct, but perhaps it wouldn't, and perhaps Goojie would consider acquiring the title worth her effort, at least to the point where she got bumped off by her own assassin.

Sula reached for her hand comm. The chronometer assured her that it was a reasonable hour in Constantinople, and she put in a call to Ratnasari.

"Lady Sula!" he said, surprise plain on his even brown features. He recovered, and his face assumed a more solemn expression. "I'm very sorry to hear about your—was she your cousin, Lady Sula?"

"Thank you," Sula said, and then watched surprise return to his face as she asked her next question. "I wonder if you have contact information for Adele Souka? The woman from Democracy Club, the one with red hair?"

Adele Souka was both startled and pleased by Sula's call. Her red hair, bright in the hand comm display, was unbound and framed her face with its thick coils. After she stammered through condolences regarding Goojie, Sula thanked her and went straight to the point.

"I was wondering if you could remind me where we met?" she asked.

Souka's surprise deepened. "Well, ah—it was at the meeting with Miss Kantari. I was her assistant."

Sula had no recollection of any such meeting, but then, she hadn't expected that she would.

"When and where was this meeting?" Sula asked.

Souka's surprise turned to bafflement. "That would be two months ago, in Adrianople." She gave a nervous smile. "Jack Danitz was so jealous I'd met you! He wanted to talk to you about tactics, and he didn't get the chance."

"He may yet," Sula muttered. "Can you tell me what the meeting was about?"

"The Kantari Modulars contract," Souka said. By now, she seemed less perplexed than deeply concerned, as if she were worried the questions could be displaying symptoms of mental illness.

"Could you refresh my memory concerning this contract?"

"Well." Souka blinked. "We make electric and communication components—modular, so they can easily be plugged in and out. And we signed a contract to supply the dockyard and all other Fleet installations with electronic components once your current contract expires." She ventured a wan smile. "We're ramping up production so that we'll be ready on the day!

And we're just about to sign an agreement on building a new assembly facility."

Sula considered this. "Were there any—" She searched for a suitable phrase. "Side agreements? Fees? Not mentioned in the contract?"

Fear touched Souka's expression. Perhaps it had occurred to her that admitting a bribe on an easily recorded video call might not be her most discrete option.

"Lady Sula? May I ask what these questions are in aid of?"

Sula decided to aim for ambiguity. "There are some discrepancies in the timeline," she said vaguely. "I'm trying to resolve them."

"Are there—" Souka tried to make sense out of Sula's answer, failed, and then apparently gave up trying to understand what was happening. She waved a hand. "The filing fees? They arrived, didn't they?"

Sula concealed the triumph that was blaring like trumpets in her head. "The person you encountered at this meeting—you'd swear she was me, yes?"

Adele Souka blinked ferociously. "I—it *was* you, Lady Sula."

"Describe her, please."

Souka's expression had grown wary. Clearly, she suspected a trap and was refusing to march blindly into it. "Well, you looked like *you*," she said. "Blonde, fair-eyed, wearing the uniform. You talked like you do, very direct."

Goojie. Sula's heart sank. She had thought she'd managed to make a friend, and instead, the woman had been planning to betray her all along.

"Thank you," Sula said. "I appreciate the information. I think you should probably tell Miss Kantari to put off acquiring that new production facility. It appears you and she have been the victims of a fraud by someone who has been impersonating me."

Souka's wary look increased. She probably thought that Sula had thought better of the Kantari deal and the bribe and was trying to wriggle out of it. Sula continued.

"You should also probably tell your firm's counsel that there will probably be a criminal investigation of the impersonator. Do you by any chance have contact information for that person? Or recall any details of the account into which the filing fees were disbursed?"

Souka had contact information, but it was useless. "I tried to contact you when I heard you were in Constantinople, but the code no longer worked."

"Thank you, Miss Souka," Sula said. "You'll get back to me with that account information, won't you?"

———

Sula's next call was to Jack Danitz. His aggressive affect

was hardly diminished by distance or by the fact that he appeared as a miniaturized, bearded bust on Sula's display. Alone of all the callers she'd received that day, Danitz did not offer condolences on Goojie's death.

"Thank you for calling, Lady Sula," he boomed in his huge baritone voice. His smile was huge. "You've decided to take me up on my offer, I assume?"

"You still haven't worked out how Light Squadron Seventeen survived Second Magaria?"

"Not yet." The brilliance of his smile faded slightly.

"Let's strike a deal, Mr. Danitz. I'll tell you how to thrash any virtual opponents at the Battle of Magaria if you'll do me a favor."

The beaming smile was back and implied that Danitz had expected exactly this situation. "Of course, Lady Sula!" he said. "What do you need?"

"I need you and your group of obsessive researchers to help me with a project."

He seemed a little surprised. "You need something researched?"

"I need someone *found.* It turns out that someone's been on Terra for at least the last couple months, impersonating me."

Danitz boomed out a laugh. "That shouldn't be a problem!"

"No?"

"Of course not! If a decorated war hero visited my town, I'd probably take a picture! And I'd put that photo in some online account where my friends could see it! And once the photo passed the censors, it would be available to practically anyone!"

Sula was dizzied by Danitz's enthusiasm. "Well," she said. "If you could tell your friends to get busy . . ."

"Of course, Lady Sula!"

A warning finger touched the back of her neck. "And if you could, caution your people to be discreet. I don't want any warning reaching this person's confederates, assuming she has any."

"Absolutely!" he roared as his presence filled the little screen. "You can count on us!"

She touched a control on her display, and the orange end-stamp filled the screen for a few seconds before the chameleon fabric rotated and returned the fabric to its normal deep green color.

Sula gave a long sigh—Danitz long-distance was nearly as exhausting as Danitz in person—and then took off her uniform tunic and returned it to the closet.

Feeling buoyed, she looked at her table and her bowl of soup, now cold, its surface spotted with shiny drops of fragrant grease, and pushed the bowl away. *I wasn't hungry, anyway,* she decided, and went to bed.

Next morning, Adele Souka sent the account number at the Bank of Zanshaa to which Kantari Modulars had sent the supposed filing fee, and Sula contacted the bank and was told that the account still existed and was in her name. Sula knew that if she had actually solicited a bribe, she would have been intelligent enough not to have put the account in her own name, and the money wouldn't have stayed there for long. But then this account was *supposed* to be found; it was *supposed* to provide evidence that would get Sula arrested and executed.

Several additional messages arrived from Jack Danitz, with pictures and video of Sula on Terra. Some were perfectly genuine, catching her in Constantinople or Xi'an, but others showed her in places where she knew she'd never been. There was also a news item describing her giving a speech to something in Paris described as "the exclusive Continental Club," the sort of event she wouldn't have attended on a bet. The quotes given in the article seemed plausible enough—they were the sort of things she might well have said had she been trapped into attending such a gathering—and they testified to the amount of research the imposter had done.

Well, there was plenty of video of her from the war that Goojie could have studied.

She messaged Danitz her thanks and told him to keep going, then studied the images of the imposter. They were uncanny—the imposter even *walked* like her, in her straight-backed military stride, and the scowl with which she regarded the video camera seemed more like Sula than Sula herself.

What the imposter didn't seem to be was Goojie. Sula couldn't see anything of Caro's cousin in the way she moved or spoke. Goojie must have been a chameleon, to have adopted Sula's part so convincingly.

Perhaps, she decided, that sort of thing ran in the family.

———

Sula's theory crumbled into dust the next morning, when Koridun delivered a report on Goojie's movements. She'd disembarked from the *Benin* exactly when she said she had, had stayed in a hotel on the ring when meeting with the Kan-fra delegates, and had then dropped to Earth to meet Sula in Sulawesi.

"Are you sure it's her?" Sula asked.

"Who else would it be, my lady?" Koridun asked. She was clearly puzzled. "I have video. Would you like to see it?"

Sula would and did. The person in the video was

clearly Goojie, smiling in the familiar way, wearing the familiar bright fabrics, walking with the familiar swinging stride. She was as much Goojie as the woman at the Continental Club had been Sula.

So, Goojie had been Goojie all along, and the imposter was someone else.

Sula was surprised at how relieved she was by the news. Goojie had been genuine, had genuinely been her friend.

"My lady?" Koridun said. "I have assembled my personnel and a group of medical and rescue techs, and we're ready to drop to Sulawesi to help secure the station and other imperial facilities from the Karangetang eruption. May we have your permission to embark?"

"Yes," Sula said, distracted. "Yes, of course."

She wondered how many *other* relatives of Caro Sula were wandering around Terra at the moment, embarked on clandestine errands.

She'd find out. But first, she had to meet with the commissioner of police.

———

Lady Gudrun Bjorge had very kindly agreed to meet Sula at the main branch of the Consolidated Bank of Zanshaa, and arrived in her grand, bemedaled uniform along with a pair of constables and the Lai-own recorder with his tablet. Sula came with Spence and Macnamara and a car loaded with firearms. The floor, ceiling, and walls of the bank were sheathed in cream-colored laminate, and the sleek desks and cabinets were a slightly darker cream color with brass accents. Sula reckoned the bank probably spent a fortune in robots keeping the place polished.

The bank manager, one Lady Oso Pai-tor, had been forewarned of their coming, and took them into her office, which featured a grand view of the Avon River, slate-gray within its banks, and brightly colored houseboats moored to the quay. The office was as brilliant white as the rest of the interior. Perched on fluted white podiums were pale porcelain flower vases filled with white lilies that filled the room with a slightly astringent scent.

Lady Oso offered refreshment, Sula accepted tea, and Lady Gudrun coffee. "I wonder if you can locate my account in your bank, Lady Oso," Sula said.

Lady Oso said that she would. Lady Oso gave verbal commands to her desk while Sula paused to admire her teacup—Guraware, from Zanshaa. Displays in the desk and on one wall brightened with new information.

"Yes," said Lady Oso. "You have an account here."

"Can you tell me when the account was opened?"

Lady Oso looked at the display. "A little over eight months ago," she said. "On Zanshaa."

Sula sipped her tea. "I *was* in the capital eight months ago. I wonder if you can tell me how much money is in the account?"

Lady Oso looked at the figures again. "Forty-five thousand, nine hundred and sixty-one zeniths, fourteen septiles."

Which was enough to live the rest of her life in very comfortable retirement, provided she stayed away from Zanshaa High City and its extravagant lifestyle. The bribes on Terra had been generous indeed.

Sula put the Guraware on the desk. "I would like to make a withdrawal, if I may," she said. "A hundred and one zeniths."

"Very good, Lady Sula." Lady Oso brushed at the feathery hair at the side of her head and gave the commands. She reached for a fingerprint reader on the desk and turned it around for Sula's use. "You'll need to give me a fingerprint."

Sula reached for the fingerprint reader and pressed her left thumb to the scanner. Symbols flashed on the displays.

"Let me clear the screen," Lady Oso said. "Then you'll have to try it again."

Sula gave her thumbprint again. The same symbols flashed.

Lady Oso's orange eyes gleamed in sudden inspiration. "You should use your *right* thumb, Lady Sula."

Sula was so pleased with herself that she wanted to purr. "I can't," she said. She held up her right thumb with its pad of scar tissue. "I severely burned my thumb just after the First Battle of Magaria, and my fingerprint was largely destroyed. So, I use my *left* thumbprint for identification." She pointed at the display. "Whoever set up this account didn't know that. They found a record of my right thumbprint somewhere and used that."

Lady Oso's muzzle gaped. Lady Gudrun sat up straight and began to look very interested.

"What are you suggesting?" she asked.

"Someone has been impersonating me on Terra for weeks now. She's been soliciting bribes for contracts related to the dockyard, and had the money delivered to this account." Sula looked at Lady Gudrun. "If you trace the origins of this money," she said, "you'll be able to discover some people trying to corrupt an officer of the Fleet."

The commissioner turned to Lady Oso. "I shall require you to freeze this account immediately."

"Of course, my lady!"

Sula retrieved her tea and sipped it while the other two expressed their outrage to each other.

She hadn't walked into this blind. Before she'd called the commissioner, she'd gone to one of the bank's remote locations and attempted and failed to access the account. She'd known beforehand that her fingerprint wouldn't work.

"You were *meant* to find the account, Lady Gudrun," she said. "I'm sure that after the assassination attempt, you were quite rightly investigating my background, and my finances would have been of obvious interest to you. And if you *hadn't* found the account, there would probably have been an anonymous denunciation."

The commissioner frowned. "Have you any idea who's responsible?"

"I've no idea. But the scheme seems to have been hatched on Zanshaa." She remembered ambushing Naxids with guns and bombs, hurling high-ranking Naxids off the cliffs of the High City, Naxid Peers without their heads staggering around in a blood-spattered room and dying slowly from shock. . . .

"I suppose," she said, "I might have made some enemies there, during the war."

Lady Gudrun pursed her lips. "Zanshaa. A little out of my jurisdiction."

"Best to find the impersonator here, then follow the trail back to the capital." She raised the display on her left sleeve. "I have information about the impersonator, and pictures. I've had researchers out looking for her, and she hasn't exactly been hiding."

In fact, Jack Danitz had delivered even more information that morning before her meeting, more appearances and sightings by the false Sula. Sula sent the data to Lady Gudrun, who paged through it with interest, then looked up.

"Whoever did this is not without resources," she said. "It's an elaborate and costly scheme, and it first required corrupting some secure source to acquire your fingerprint, and then the technical knowledge to duplicate it well enough to spoof a fingerprint reader."

"There are special films you can put over your thumb," Sula said. "Or so I learned from the *Doctor An-ku Mysteries*."

"True enough," said Lady Gudrun. "But it's beyond the skill level of the average criminal." She looked thoughtful. "As is everything else in this setup."

"Except the assassin."

"Except the assassin," Lady Gudrun repeated. She turned to Lady Oso. "I'm sorry, my lady, but Lady Sula and I should really continue this in private. Is there a room we could use?"

"You can use my office." Lady Oso rose. "Is there anything I can get you before I leave?"

"I think we have everything we need," Lady Gudrun said, and as Lady Oso made her way out, added, "*Tēnā rawa atu koe.*"

"*Noho ora mai,*" Lady Oso said, and closed the door behind her.

Is everyone *a Maori here?* Sula wondered. Even the nonhumans?

Lady Gudrun turned to Sula. "What do you suppose the conspirators are after?" she asked.

"They want me disgraced and possibly executed," Sula said.

"*Disgraced,*" Lady Gudrun said. "That's the main point. If they merely wanted you dead, they'd have just sent the assassin, possibly more than one. Who hates you so much they're willing to spend a lot of money to destroy your *reputation?*"

The Supreme Commander, for one, Sula thought, but she decided not to speak the thought out loud. Besides, Lord Tork was far too conventional and stuffy to engage in a complex revenge plot, not when he'd already won simply by sending Sula to a remote station.

"Naxids, I suppose," Sula said. "I can't imagine anyone else."

"Do you still think the Manado Company is involved? Or have we eliminated them?"

This thought hadn't occurred to Sula, and it took her a moment to formulate a response. "Lord Peltrot's threats shouldn't be forgotten," she decided. "He may have played a part in this somewhere. Maybe he bribed the imposter, then tried to kill me when I didn't fulfill her half of the bargain."

"We'll continue to look at him, then," said Lady Gudrun. "But right now, I'd like to institute a search for this imposter." Her mouth tightened in a self-satisfied little smile. "If she's on the planet, we'll find her."

Now, *that* was the sort of thing Sula liked to hear.

———

The rest of the morning was spent coping with the matter of Goojie's servants, who up to that point had been completely forgotten. There had been the female valet in Otautahi, but there was also a whole gang of domestics and secretaries sent to staff Goojie's lodgings in Quito. None of them wanted to stay on Terra, and while Sula felt a certain degree of responsibility to them, she didn't feel responsible to the point of buying passage home for the entire group. Fortunately, she remembered that the Vaswanis were clients of the Toi-an clan, and a brief search turned up an elderly Toi-an Peer who had preceded Goojie as director of the Kan-fra Company, and who had retired to a Caribbean island. He agreed to assume responsibility for the servants, and to either send them home or find employment for them.

Which led Sula's thoughts to Goojie. Caro's cousin

wasn't a conspirator. She hadn't come to Terra to destroy Sula; she had been a victim, not a mastermind, of the plot to disgrace Sula—more of a victim than Sula, in fact.

And apparently, she'd been Sula's friend. Sula felt a pang of relief at this realization, at the knowledge that someone had been her friend, that friendship was even *possible* in her world, filled as it was with shifting identities, violence, military action, treachery, and conspiracy. . . .

Sula could have friends. Somehow, Goojie had given her permission.

Of course, that still meant she'd have to *find* some.

These pleasant thoughts were interrupted by a call from Lady Gudrun Bjorge. "*Kia ora!*" she said in triumph. "We've found her!"

"Where?"

"Three hours ago, she got off a train from Manado to Tambu, in Sulawesi. She's traveling under the name Tamlin Sage, which sounds like a pseudonym to me."

"She's heading for the elevator, then," Sula said. "We can arrest her at the terminal."

"I've already given the order, but she may not turn up. Traffic to the ring has been halted on account of anticipated volcanic activity. All the cars have been sent up to the ring to prevent them from being damaged."

Damn, Sula thought; she kept forgetting about the

Karangetang volcano. But she seized the important point at once. "She's trapped," Sula said.

"Yes." There was satisfaction in the commissioner's voice. "I believe she is." There was a pause, and she added, "It may take some time to locate her. The town is flooded with refugees from Manado, and there may not be rooms available for her. If she's in a refugee center, they may not be checking ID."

"I need to get to Tambu," Sula said. "What's the fastest way?"

Lady Gudrun gave her an amused look. "You wish to meet yourself?"

"I damned well do. I need to find out who employed her."

"The police commissioner is entitled to a small aircraft," Lady Gudrun said. "You're welcome to use it. But it can't stay for you; all aircraft and ships are being routed away."

"Thank you," said Sula, "for your generous offer."

———————

Lady Gudrun's plane wasn't as swank as Goojie's Kanfra craft, but it had a polite uniformed attendant who provided a wonderful fragrant tea from the highlands of Washington State, wherever that was. Once airborne,

Sula called Lieutenant-Captain Koridun in Tambu and told her she was coming.

"You're going to take command, my lady?" Sula sensed calculation behind Koridun's eyes. On the one hand, she might resent being superseded after she'd made preparations for the emergency on her own. And on the other, there would be a chance to have her readiness and efficiency appreciated directly by a superior officer.

"If the emergency is bad, we may need every officer we can find," Sula said. "Do we have a probability of the eruption?"

"Specialists have stated there *will* be an eruption, Lady Sula," said Koridun. "Any time within the next thirty-six Terran hours. The Lord Governor has just declared martial law."

"All your people are in place?"

"Yes, Lady Sula."

"Are there any problems I can help you with?"

"Not unless you can bring a few thousand more police and aid workers. Tambu is overrun with refugees, and because the elevator terminus is one of the largest and most stable buildings, it's completely full except for a few offices and the armory. No one is being disorderly on purpose, but there's a lot of confusion, the sanitary facilities are overtaxed, and I don't know if I'll be able to feed everyone, or for how long."

"Call for refugee volunteers to help maintain order, cook, and keep things clean. The refugees will be bored, so you'll have plenty of recruits who just want to be given something to do."

"Yes, my lady."

Sula considered the problem. "The public areas have video monitors, yes? Reporting on the cars coming down from the ring, times of boarding, and so on?"

"Yes, my lady."

"There are no cars coming down, so there's no point in showing them a screen without information. See if you can switch them to a news feed of the volcano. When it blows, they're going to be riveted to the screens, and there will be that much less chaos."

Koridun seemed impressed. "Very good, my lady."

"I'll be dropping in about fifty minutes. Please have a pair of guards waiting for me at the pier, with a vehicle."

"Yes, my lady. At once."

No sooner had the orange end-stamp appeared on Sula's display than a chime announced another call, this time from the police commissioner. Sula triggered her display.

"*Kia ora,* Lady Gudrun. Is there more news?"

"*Kia ora,* yes. The imposter's been shown checking into the UnderSea Hotel in the Gulf of Tomini."

"Under the rectenna field?"

"Yes."

Sula was surprised. "Can ordinary persons go down there? It's underwater and we're on the cusp of a natural disaster. I would have thought the place would be evacuated."

Lady Gudrun gave a tight-lipped smile. "She used your identity, Lady Sula."

"Ah. Hah."

"They're not about to keep out an officer of your distinction, especially as during emergencies, the Power Authority is under the control of the Fleet."

"I'll give her credit for being resourceful," Sula said. "But in impersonating me now, she's just condemned herself. Can you arrange with your opposite number in Tambu to have her arrested?"

"I'll ask. But the police may be a bit . . . overcommitted . . . right now."

"I understand."

Nevertheless, the imposter *was* arrested before Sula's plane landed: there was a skeleton police force patrolling the underwater resort, and it took mere moments for them to detour to the hotel and the imposter's room. The prisoner was locked in the resort's small jail and awaited either Sula or a magistrate, whoever arrived first.

The aircraft dropped through low cloud to a landing in Tambu's bay, white water rising high as the plane skipped along the wavetops. When the sea sluiced off the windows, Sula could see the city glowing red with the setting sun, with the monumental structure of the elevator terminal rising from the heights behind the town. The craft motored to the government pier, where a pair of large, fully manned rescue craft were prepared for departure. A gantry swung toward the aircraft, and the hatch opened, letting in a gust of sultry equatorial air scented with the sea. Sula felt herself sag in the sudden heat.

Her vehicle—a boxy van—and her escort awaited her on the pier, two Fleet constables, both Terran, in armor and carrying sidearms. They hastened to snatch up the baggage from Spence and Macnamara, and nearly hurled it into the back of the vehicle. Sula was about to embark when she suddenly felt her knees tremble, and she reached out a hand to the vehicle to steady herself only to find that the van itself was bouncing on its suspension. The surface of the ocean leaped as if in an invisible downpour. Macnamara, carrying a trunk, was suddenly unbalanced and staggered over the pier. One of the escort reached out a hand to stop him from going in the drink.

The tremor faded. Sula's head spun. Her heart was in her throat.

"We've been feeling those the last two days, my lady," said one of the escort. "I'd like to drive out of the tsunami zone as soon as possible. The whole lower town's been evacuated."

"Let's go, then," Sula said, and, as soon as she felt steady enough, climbed into the seat. The rear hatch rattled down on the baggage, everyone climbed in and found their seats, and the vehicle sped away down deserted streets. Sula looked over her shoulder at the sunset—all lurid Earth color, nothing like any sunset seen on Zanshaa—and then the van was climbing.

"We're going to the terminal, my lady?" said the driver.

"No. We're going over to the east side of the island to pick up a prisoner, in Tinombala."

The two escorts looked at each other, and the van accelerated on silent electric motors.

———

The tropical darkness fell quickly, and the van raced along a highway deserted but for emergency vehicles awaiting the inevitable destruction. The road passed through suburbs and villages where only the schools and other public buildings were lit, to accommodate all the locals as refugees. "The whole island's on battery power," the driver said. "The rectenna's been shut down."

It took only a short time to cross the peninsula to the eastern shore, and then the car turned north with Tomini

Bay to the right. The receivers of the rectenna field were equipped with yellow blinking lights to mark the navigation hazard, and the sea looked like a vast meadow filled with fireflies, gently undulating up and down.

"We're back in the tsunami zone," the driver said, his tone of voice indicating that he very much disapproved of being there.

"Isn't there a whole peninsula between us and the volcano?" Sula asked. "How's a tsunami going to reach us?"

"The tremors could set off a more conventional earthquake, my lady, under the sea somewhere. You see—"

And then Sula's eyes were dazzled by an enormous flash to the northeast, a searing light that glared off the low cloud cover. Everything that wasn't in deep shadow turned to blazing fire. "Oh hell that's it," said the driver.

Sula remembered the antimatter weapons the Shaa had dropped on Zanshaas's suburb of Remba, the flash followed by the furious concussion that sent roofs flying and turned windows into shrapnel.

"Careful of the shock wave!" she called to the driver. "Slow down, make sure we're not under anything that can fall . . ."

Then it was on them, visible at the last instant as a great dark pall rushing down the highway, enveloping as a shroud. There was a sharp cracking sound like the biggest bullwhip in the world, and pain in the ears that made

Sula cry out and slap her hands to the side of her head. Something snatched the breath from her throat. Tires screamed as the slab-sided vehicle was picked up and tossed back down the road. The van's windows turned all to stars, and then the windscreen was battered by an airborne swarm of tree branches, stones, gravel, chunks of pavement, anything the shock wave had picked up as it flew along. . . . The windscreen caved in, and the van's interior was flooded with humid tropical air bearing a cargo of leaves, twigs, and other debris. Sula covered her face in self-defense. There was a strong odor of vegetation.

The driver had been blasted back in his seat, but the van's safety mechanisms took over, and though the vehicle rocked and swayed, it stayed upright. The vegetable torrent abated, leaving the van's passengers gasping and spitting out leaves and twigs, and then the van bounced again as the ground wave passed beneath them.

Ahead was a hellish dawn, the horizon a vivid scarlet reflected by the clouds. Loud cracks and booms echoed through the trees.

Sula wiped grit from her face. "Is everyone all right?" she asked.

The driver was bleeding from both ears and reeling with vertigo; Spence punched out what remained of the window and took his place. No one else had been subjected to more than a minor cut. "Get on to Tinombala," Sula said. "There will be an aid center or a hospital, I'm sure."

The vehicle lurched into motion, weaving between fallen trees and branches. The red glow ahead waxed and waned. The air was dark and seemed to press in on all sides. More towns, more villages, broken glass and fallen signs. A large rescue boat powered along offshore, brightly lit, seemingly undamaged. And then, right in the road, a police vehicle that had fared less well than their own. It had turned over, and its emergency lights flashed dimly in the choked air. Spence drew the van alongside.

Both police were cut and bleeding and shaken, and also knew where the emergency clinic had been set up in Tinombala's town hall, fortunately situated above any likely tsunami line. Sula took the stranded police aboard and got them to the clinic, where they also unloaded the former driver with his blown eardrums.

Looming above Tinombala's darkened streets was a rearing, spotlit monolith, the access to the tunnel that led to the rectenna's control room and the UnderSea Hotel. Spence brought the van to a halt under a scalloped concrete portico, and they disembarked to find the doors locked. Spence pressed the button, Macnamara banged on the door, and Sula called the underwater police station.

A hissing rose from the air around them. Something began to fall on the portico with the sound of softly sifting sand. Granules of ash, sighing down from the black, featureless sky.

Macnamara's tactic worked, and an elderly Lai-own security guard opened the door. Her feathery hair had thinned to nearly nothing, revealing gray skin, and she walked with the mincing step peculiar to decrepit, footsore avians. "I was told you'd be coming," she said. "Looks like you were lucky to make it."

Sula stepped inside and was relieved to find the air cool and free of particulates. Her shoes echoed in a vast empty atrium only dimly glimpsed in the emergency lighting. She brushed dust from her tunic.

The building shook to another ground wave. Something metallic rattled overhead.

"I can put you on the train leading down below the bay," the guard said. "There are only a few people down there, a couple at the hotel, a few police, and a small group at the power control station." She offered Sula a sage nod. "Things go wrong, there's a submarine escape vehicle at the power station. They'll take you off."

"Perhaps you'd better tell me how to find it," Sula said.

"You can download a map to your hand comm," the guard continued serenely, as if unaware of the interruption. "It will guide you where you need to go. I shall call the police and have them meet you at the station."

Sula's remaining constable spoke up. He was tall and fit, but his face under the smears of dust was pale, and dried blood smeared his chin. "Lady Captain? Are we actually going into an underwater structure? With earthquakes and an eruption going on?"

"Yes, we are," said Sula. She turned to the Lai-own. "The designers of the facility knew full well that earthquakes and volcanoes were a possibility, did they not?"

The serene voice resumed. "Oh, yes, my lady. The structure is built to resist earthquake . . . and then of course there's the submarine if there's trouble."

Sula turned back to the constable. "We've known for millennia how to build pressurized compartments. I flew here in one, all the way from Zanshaa." She tried to look reassuring. "We won't be long. We're just going to pick up a prisoner."

The constable took a deep breath and visibly steeled himself. "Very well, my lady."

They followed the mincing Lai-own to the train station, triggered their sleeve displays to download a map of the facility, then took their places in a small, roofless electric tram car. When the tram started with a jerk, Sula couldn't be sure if the jolt was the train or another shock.

Subdued emergency lighting lit the long tunnel, which was painted with gay figures of whatever creatures might be found at the appropriate depth, starfish and urchins near the surface, then down through parrot fish and eels and angels, turtles, jacks, sharks, and squid. The decorations would have been charming had they been seen in daylight, but in the near-darkness, they seemed shadowy, ominous figures, mostly teeth and eyes, inhabiting a dark, oppressive realm.

At the train station a Naxid police sergeant waited, his four feet planted on the platform, motionless as an equestrian statue. Sula's hackles rose at the sight of an armed Naxid looming up out of the darkness, but at her appearance, the sergeant braced to attention and waited for the party to disembark.

"My lady," he said. "May I escort you to the prisoner?"

"You may."

The community's little jail was a two-minute walk away, over paving stones carved from limestone, with visible impressions of seashells, fish, and aquatic plants. The roof was so far above that it was invisible. The resort looked eerie in the darkness, the hotel dark save for a glowing NO VACANCY sign; tables and chairs disordered at a sidewalk cafe; the seahorses, crabs, and sharks of an aquatic-themed merry-go-round lying still, listless eyes gazing into the void. Vertigo skated through Sula's head from the almost-continual jolts.

A police cadet, another Naxid, waited at the police station. "I've run the prisoner's fingerprints," she reported. "She's Anna Servilia Spendlove, originally of Chijimo. Seven years ago, she was indicted for fraud and theft, but the charges weren't pressed, apparently because she informed on her accomplices. She was indicted two years later, for some kind of insurance fraud, but she skipped to Zanshaa ahead of the warrant, and she later turned up selling forged art under the name Costanza Vole. Again she escaped conviction, because her victims wouldn't testify against her."

"Why wouldn't they?" Sula asked.

"We have to worry about confidence tricksters here at the resort," the sergeant said. "They're charming and make good friends of their victims—and often, their victims like them so much, they refuse to hurt them by testifying."

"Or," Macnamara added cynically, "the victims don't want to admit to being fooled or admit that their art isn't worth as much as they paid for it."

"Is there a photo?" Sula asked. "May I see it?"

The picture was in three dimensions, and Sula could spin it to different angles with the touch of a finger. Anna Servilia Spendlove had a mass of dark corkscrew curls, brown eyes, and an attractive, intelligent face with a complexion several shades darker than Sula's. The photo had been taken at her most recent arraignment, and she was overdressed for the occasion in a high-collared gown of some shiny dark red fabric, worn with just a touch of defiance. It looked as if she'd been arrested at a premiere at the Oh-lo-ho Theater in Zanshaa High City.

It would have taken work, and money, to turn Spendlove into Sula, but then, the whole scheme reeked of money. Just whose money was the important question.

"I would like to see the prisoner alone," she said. "Or, rather, in the company of my own constable."

The sergeant was all agreement. "As your ladyship wishes."

Anna Spendlove was alone in a surprisingly large steel-walled room, painted a dreary dark gray—from the sharp smell of disinfectant and the oversized drain in the center of the room, Sula realized it was a drunk tank. Drunken tourists, she supposed, were probably the most common business of the police. There were toilets suitable for all species and a dim light covered by a grate.

Spendlove was lying on a metal shelf, and at the sound of the door opening, she sat up, blinking at the shadowy forms in the doorway. Sula's pale gold hair framed Spendlove's face. She wasn't dressed as a Fleet officer but instead wore a dark blue blouse and cream-colored trousers, all suitable for a tourist on a tropical vacation. Sula stepped into the room's dim light, and she saw the shock on Spendlove's face as she recognized her visitor.

Sula also recognized a face, the one turned up to her, Caro returned from the dead and all grown up. Sula felt her throat clench, her heart give a lurch.

As if waiting for an appropriate dramatic moment, a temblor rocked the room, and all the metal beds rattled on their hinges. Water slopped out of the toilet.

Sula saw Spendlove blot the surprise from her face and craft a new, critical look to replace it.

"You look like hell," she said.

Sula took a breath, let it out, tried to quell the pulse hammering in her throat. She groped in her mind for the questions she'd planned to ask Spendlove, and could remember none of them. But it was clear that Spendlove was trying to control the conversation, and that Sula couldn't let her.

"You look like a dead woman," Sula said. Caro's face, worn by Spendlove, twisted in annoyance, and then opened its mouth to speak.

Sula took a step closer to the prisoner, and to keep from fidgeting, she clasped her hands behind her back. She looked down at Caro's face and forced herself to remember she was facing an enemy, someone part of a scheme to kill her. No better than the Naxids she'd killed in the war.

"There's a major volcanic eruption just north of here," she said. "Thousands of people are going to be dead by sunrise. There's martial law, and anyone caught in the commission of a crime can be executed." She unclasped one hand and formed it into the shape of a gun. She pointed a forefinger at Spendlove, and another memory floated up, pointing the finger at herself in the bathroom mirror just after Goojie's death. *That's what this is about,* she'd thought. *And this is who I am.*

She wondered how often she'd have to kill Caro, and thought this might not be the last time.

"I can shoot you right between those phony green eyes," she told Spendlove. She gave a glance at the drain set into the floor. "There's even an oversized drain for your blood."

Spendlove's eyes flickered. Sula had shaken her confidence, but she tried to summon something like defiance.

"I haven't hurt you," she said. "I'm the one in jail, not you."

"Tell that to my cousin Lady Ermina Vaswani."

"I had nothing to do with any killing. I didn't do it, and I didn't know about it."

Sula put her gun hand behind her back. "I can do worse than shoot you," she said. Spendlove's eyes flickered again. Sula permitted a tight smile to touch her mouth. "The fraud you've perpetrated was aimed at corrupting Fleet contracts, and a crime against the government is a crime against the Praxis—which means I can turn you over to the Legion of Diligence for interrogation and the most appalling execution you can imagine."

Spendlove couldn't conceal the look of horror that flashed across her face. "I didn't harm the Fleet," she said quickly. "I didn't take a single minim from the government. I only dealt with contractors."

Sula tried to look skeptical. "You could certainly make that argument," she said. "But in my experience, the Legion is very reluctant to return cases to the civil authority."

Spendlove took a breath, straightened, and put her hands on her thighs like a schoolgirl sitting obediently at her desk. "I'll tell you what you want to know," she said, "if you'll agree to leave me in the custody of the civil police."

"That depends on the quality of the information," Sula said. "If it can't be authenticated, I'll have to bring the Legion in."

"I'll tell you everything," Spendlove said.

Sula didn't bother to hide her triumph. She flexed her hands behind her back. "All right, then," she said. "Who's behind this? A Naxid clan?"

Spendlove blinked up in surprise. "Naxids?" she said. "No. Everyone I dealt with was Torminel."

Sula stared at her. And then, at that moment, the jail took a violent leap to one side, jumping right out from under Sula's feet, and the lights went out.

———————

The two Naxid police arrived with battery lights, just after a mild alarm had begun bleating. The door was opened, the lights shone in, and the sergeant said, "That is a decompression warning. We should evacuate."

Sula had already felt the pressure in her ears. She gulped and the pressure faded.

"Secure the prisoner first," she said.

Macnamara handcuffed Anna Spendlove and the party moved at speed out of the police station. The bleating was louder once they got onto the main concourse. Spotlights high on the invisible ceiling strobed red and green on the limestone street.

"Follow the green," the sergeant said. "The red leads to the resort's tourist submarines, and those have been removed to a safer location."

Sula felt pressure building in her ears. "Better run," she said. "We'll follow you!"

The Naxids needed no urging: they sped off along the greenlit path with the ferocious clattering velocity of their species, whipping along while using all six limbs, and the Terrans followed as quickly as they could. Sula had to keep pinching her nose to clear her ears.

Sula wondered how many atmospheres were building up in this place. To compress the air this much, a truly

vast amount of water must be coming in, and she wondered where it all was. Beneath them? Were there corri-
dors and storerooms and basements below her feet, all
now swimming with water?

The Naxid police ran to a green door marked with
the symbol of the Power Services Authority, yanked it
open, and dashed inside. Sula followed. She found herself in a bleak utilitarian corridor of pale yellow, decorated by nondescript photographs of the receiver complex and various underwater creatures found in the vicin-
ity. As she ran, broad windows opened up on the left,
and she saw benches, screens, and readouts, the rectenna
field's control room. The Naxids ignored the control
room and banged through a door at the end of the hall.
The path turned right for a moment, then through a
swinging door that led to a steel-grill deck overlooking
a large metal-walled room. Lockers lined the walls, and
equipment lay on racks.

For the first time, Sula saw water; it was ankle-deep
in the room and bubbling up from somewhere below
the floor. There was an overwhelming organic
reek—seawater, sea plants, sea muck. A metal stair led
from the deck to the floor below, and the Naxids ran
down it without hesitation, their boots splashing in
the dark water that covered the floor. When Sula followed them down the stair, she saw where they were

running: under the deck was a pressure door to some kind of self-contained environment, possibly an airlock. It was shut, but a Terran, a man she'd never seen, was trying to tug the door open.

She leaped into the water. It was shockingly cold and already to her knees. A temblor nearly threw her into the water and caused the surface to leap. There was a clang, and Sula looked up to see Spendlove, still handcuffed, nearly topple down the stair, until Macnamara grabbed her shoulder and steadied her. And then she heard Spence give a cry, and turned to see water pouring through the door she'd just run through, gushing onto the decking and falling like rain through the grill, onto the man struggling with the airlock door.

The water was to Sula's waist by the time the Naxid police and two strong Terran men finally wrenched the airlock door open, fighting against the pressure both of water and air until both the air and water equalized. The party piled in—the airlock was large enough for thirty people—and the door was swung shut and sealed.

The Terrans stood waist-deep in water, gasping. The bodies of the centauroid Naxids were almost entirely submerged, with only their arms, shoulders, and heads above water. The alarm blared off the enameled metal walls and a long row of lockers and hatches and overhead rails for equipment. Gaudy displays urged them to evac-

uate and follow emergency procedure. The water leaped
to a series of tremors.

"Can we pump this room out?" Sula asked, raising her
voice over the alarm.

"If there's enough emergency power," said the
sergeant. He began scanning the lock's control menu,
found an appropriate page, pushed a button. A mechanical throb began, interrupted occasionally by a throat-clearing sound.

Sula cleared her ears. "What's the air pressure in here?"
she asked.

The police cadet looked at gauges. "Five point one at-mospheres, my lady," she said. She reached for a control.
"I can bleed off all the extra."

"*No!*" Everyone in the Fleet shouted the word in uni-son. The cadet not only withdrew her arm but jumped
back from the controls.

"It has to be done slowly," Sula explained. "Or we'll all
get the bends."

Agony, convulsions, and death, Sula thought, while
the blood turns to the consistency of clotted cream. *Not*
a part of the plan.

"Yes, my lady," the cadet said, a bit primly.

"Where's the blasted submarine?" said the strange
Terran. He was a dark-skinned man, small enough that
the water came to his armpits, and he wore an elaborate

turquoise uniform jacket with the badge of the UnderSea Hotel. He half-swam through the murky water toward another airlock door on the far side of the room, then peered at the airlock controls. He gave an angry shrug at the readout, then jabbed at a video screen. It showed nothing but blackness.

"Submarine's gone!" he said.

Sula shivered in the cold water. She was trying to work out how long it would take to slowly purge the extra atmosphere from the room. She and Fleet enlisted would have trained on vacuum suits, and much of the training was done in water tanks, though hardly at five atmospheres. She had memorized charts and tables and formulae, but most of it had to do with exposure to the vacuum of space, not cold murky seawater five atmospheres down.

Sula decided to abandon that for a moment and bobbed through the water to join the angry Terran at the hatch for the submarine.

"The bastards have abandoned us!" the man said. "They were supposed to wait!"

"Is there a way of contacting the sub?"

The man waved his hands hopelessly at the controls. "I've no idea! I work for the hotel; I'm not a damned submariner!"

Sula paged through the menu, found the controls for

the underwater speakers and hydrophone, activated the system, and began speaking.

"Base to submarine. Base to submarine. We have seven survivors waiting for pickup. We have survivors. Respond, please."

Sula waited for a response while the compartment shivered to a series of quakes, and then repeated the signal. To her surprise, an answer came, a melodious Daimong voice speaking with surprising clarity. The submarine was very near.

"This is the *Dyak III*. We can't moor to a compromised structure. It's too hazardous."

The chiming voice was so beautiful that the discouraging message seemed worse by comparison.

"*Dyak III*," Sula said, "we have seven waiting for pickup."

The answer was less melodious. "The entire complex has been knocked off its foundations by an avalanche. The building's coming apart. I'm not going anywhere near it."

Anger sang through Sula as she carefully composed her next message. "*Dyak III*, I hereby officially inform you that martial law is now in place, and the Fleet has been placed in command of all government facilities. This is Captain the Lady Sula, and I *order* you to dock with this station."

There was a long pause, as if the submarine's crew were conferring. Then: "Your message was garbled, miss. Please repeat."

Helplessly, Sula repeated the message. She was tempted to add *Return or I'll personally shoot you,* but on reflection decided that it was pointless to threaten someone who held all the cards.

"Your message was garbled," came the answer. "We are unable to understand or comply. We are moving further away from the station for the safety of our craft."

Sula called again, asking for a response, but got nothing.

"That was fucking precious," came a voice that was surprisingly like her own. "That was a piece of tactical brilliance, that was." Sula turned to see Anna Spendlove in the middle of the airlock, looking at her, her old arrogance back. Spendlove sneered, her straight-backed posture mirroring Sula's own bearing. "At least we die together. You can hardly threaten me now."

Sula looked at her. "We could push you over and find out how well you can swim when handcuffed. Want to give it a try?"

Spendlove decided not to respond and turned her head away, as if Sula wasn't worthy of her attention. Sula saw that the water level had fallen to her mid-thigh, so at least the pumps were working, if slower than she would have liked. She turned to the angry Terran.

"Is there any other way off the station?"

"Escape capsules," the man said. "Which I don't trust, because I know too well how everything in this place has been maintained."

"Well," Sula said. "We'd better find out."

"My lady." Spence called from across the room. "We've got the algorithm for decompression. It's built into the system. We can start relieving pressure."

"Do it," Sula said. *And hope the valves work the way they're designed and don't let in more water.*

"We need to tell the system how long we've been at this pressure," Spence said.

Sula's mind went blank. "Ten minutes?" she said. "Better make it fifteen for safety's sake."

Spence turned back to a control panel and punched in orders. There was no immediate sensation of air pressure dropping, but Spence peered at the display and said, "Depressurization commencing, my lady."

"Can you turn off that damned alarm? I can't think."

"I'll see what I can do."

Sula shivered again. The stink of the ocean bottom clogged her senses. She decided she needed to work out an escape before hypothermia stole her reason.

She turned to the display and paged through to the escape procedures, and discovered that the escape capsules were right there, attached to the airlock. The displays that would otherwise have marked them were instead flashing commands to evacuate, without mentioning that this was where everyone was to evacuate *to*.

Sula called up instructions. There were eight capsules altogether, each of which could hold up to six humanoids or four Naxids. When the capsule was ready to launch, it would release a buoy to the surface on a cable, where it would start broadcasting an emergency signal. When released, the capsule itself would bob up the cable to the surface.

Macnamara had been rummaging in the lockers. "My lady," he said. "Look at this."

He held out a helmet and the upper portion of what looked like a suit of armor, white laminate with red stripes. Sula looked at it and laughed.

"That's more like it!" She sloshed through the water—it came only to her knees now—and examined the suit. It was very close to a Fleet vac suit, with similar controls and a self-contained fuel supply with a rebreather. The hardsuit had little water jets for maneuver, and gossamer fins that could be deployed from the boots. The power pack registered full.

"How many of them are there?"

They found four suits suitable for humanoids, each numbered, each striped in a different color, each with a full power pack. Two would fit Naxids, but neither of the police had been trained in their use. Also in the lockers was a variety of tools, some of them clearly intended for a single purpose, to be used outside in maintaining the structure.

"Right," Sula said. "One for each member of the Fleet."

"And the rest of us will drown, I suppose," said Anna Spendlove.

Sula looked at her. "The rest of you will go up in one of the capsules."

Everyone froze in place as the small room shuddered and then was filled with the sound of a horrific rending, like a steel wall slowly being torn in two by a giant. There followed a boom, very close, and then there was a sinister scraping sound, as if a piece of sharp metal was being drawn deliberately along the side of the lock.

"This place is utter shit," said the angry man. Everyone remembered to breathe.

The alarm cut off in mid-chirp. Sula looked at Spence, who was still at the control panel. "Did you do that?"

"I don't think so, my lady."

That could be better, she thought. "Better get you loaded into the capsules and away," she decided.

But they had to wait. The hatches to the capsules were partly submerged, and the difference in water and air pressure kept them from opening. There was only one fragile-seeming handle on each hatch, and Sula didn't want to apply too much force. So, Sula and the other Fleet personnel hauled the hardsuits out of their lockers and hung the components from the overhead bars intended for the purpose. Sula was cheered by the activity—it kept her from freezing, and though she hated the claustrophobic closeness of a vac suit, at least the diving suits could maneuver freely instead of bobbing on the end of a cable, a sure invitation to seasickness.

"My lady?" It was the constable who'd met her on the pier. His face was pale, a contrast to the blood trickling from flying windshield cuts. "My vac suit training was a little . . . rudimentary, and a long time ago. Maybe I'd better take one of the capsules."

"Very good. You can escort the prisoner."

A relieved sigh visibly heaved the constable's chest. "Thank you, my lady."

There was a chime from the lock's console, and Spence looked at the readout. "Decompression's over. We're at one atmosphere, my lady."

"About time."

"There's a recommendation that we breathe pure oxygen for ten minutes to clear the last of the nitrogen out of our systems."

Sula gave a skeletal grin. "Anyone found an oxygen tank?"

No one had. The water was now ankle-deep, though

the footing remained treacherous. Sula got one of the capsule doors open, put her head through the narrow opening, and looked at the egg-shaped interior space. There was a narrow bench that ran around the inside, and otherwise a couple windows, some simple controls, and the smell of mildew. She withdrew her head.

"Right," she said. "First three."

That would be Spendlove, the constable, and the angry civilian. The constable entered first, helped the handcuffed Spendlove to enter without damaging herself, and then the angry man crawled in last.

"Do not launch until you have the light telling you that the buoy's reached the surface," Sula said.

"Yes, my lady," said the constable.

"If the buoy hasn't deployed fully, you could be caught partway up the cable and there'd be no way to free you."

"Very good, my lady."

Sula shut the door and heard the clink of the constable triggering the door's locking bolts. She stood and watched the display, and heard a rasping noise, a clank, more rasping that faded to a hiss, and then nothing.

"Buoy's away," Spence said. They waited for the light that would indicate the buoy had reached the surface, but it didn't flash.

"Negative function," said Spence.

"Right," said Sula. She turned to the Naxid police.

"Into the next capsule. We'll pull these other people out."

The Naxids climbed into the next capsule in the row, closed the door, and deployed the buoy in the time it took for the three Terrans to clamber out of the first capsule.

"Negative function." Again the buoy deployed but apparently never reached the surface.

"Negative function."

"Negative function."

The first five capsules all had the same problem. The last three buoys wouldn't release at all.

"I *told* you the maintenance here is for shit!" said the angry man.

Sula glared at the last of the capsules' control panels and considered kicking it. Her run of ill luck seemed absurd and extreme, as if some malevolent god of chance had its thumb on the scales.

Avalanche. How many people died in underwater avalanches?

Instead of lashing out, she gathered in a sodden circle with Spence and Macnamara. "The cable's fouled, or the buoy's stuck on something," she said. "We're going to have to go outside and fix it."

Only Macnamara made an effort to look optimistic. "Yes, my lady."

"I'll go out first," Sula said. "I'll analyze the problem

and tell you what sort of tools you might need to bring with you."

Sula threw off her tunic and kicked off her sodden shoes, and Spence and Macnamara helped her enter the hardsuit and adjusted the internal webbing to her body. She hoisted herself up to one of the overhead bars and dropped her feet and legs into the lower part. Boots were placed over her feet and locked on at the shins. She knelt to make it easier for Macnamara and Spence to drop the upper body on her, and then staggered to her feet while the others steadied her. She now weighed twice as much as she normally did, and even though the extra weight was distributed evenly, she was glad for the support of the others.

Claustrophobia's clammy fingers closed round her throat as the helmet was locked onto its ring. Her senses filled with the scent of the suit seals, her own wet clothing, the muck she'd stepped in. She kept focused on the business of bringing the suit to life, watching the lights on the head-up display as they ran through their changes.

"Suit's nominal," Sula said. "Can you hear me?"

"Barely, my lady," said Macnamara.

Sula manipulated the controls on her left arm, paging through menus until she found the commands for the external acoustics. "Is this better?" she asked.

Macnamara and Spence winced at the volume. "Yes."

"Someone stand by on the hydrophone," Sula said, "and relay my instructions."

The entire room served as an airlock for the submarine, but the airlock had another airlock for divers. It was small, and Sula had to get on hands and knees to crawl into it. Spence and Macnamara kept her from toppling and closed the hatch behind.

Claustrophobia threatened to smother her. She turned on the suit lights to relieve the darkness and the fear, and did so just in time for water to start gushing in, a tidal wave powered by five atmospheres of pressure. Sula closed her eyes and concentrated on calming her breath while the black tide battered her faceplate and the seawater rose around her.

Water filled the chamber, and the outer door opened. Sula could see nothing but blackness beyond. She moved forward with crabbing motions of her knees and elbows, and then drifted free. She clamped one hand on the rim of the lock and bobbed in the weightless silence. The only sound in the suit was the gasping of her own breath, the sound of her panicked pulse in her ears.

"Lady Sula?" came an amplified voice, that of the angry hotel man. "Lady Sula? Are you all right?"

Sula gulped air and tried to suppress the fear that was breathing in her face. "I'm fine," she said. "I'm trying to get oriented. Send out Macnamara next."

Around her was darkness, not a hint of a light anywhere but on her suit, the floodlight atop her helmet and another light on her right wrist. The water was murky, filled with swirling turbidity, and with what looked like falling black snow. She stared, wiped her faceplate with a hand, and still saw the black specks drifting down.

Volcanic ash from Karangetang, each particle no larger than a grain of sand, all raining slowly to the bottom of the bay. The ash fell against her faceplate without a sound, tracked snakelike across it.

Sula felt the tug of a current. She tried to orient herself by panning the wrist light over and above. Scaffolding hung in the darkness, pale alloy crossbeams forming some kind of open structure. She lowered the light and saw the escape capsules nested in their sleeves like eggs in a container at the market, then tracked the buoy cables upward and saw them disappear into the scaffolding.

She released and armed the joystick on the inside of her right wrist, then made a tentative attempt to maneuver with the impellers. The movement was too sudden and violent and nearly threw her into the structure. Suddenly, it seemed more desirable to swim.

She triggered the fins and kicked toward the scaffolding overhead. The suit defaulted to neutral buoyancy, and the swimming seemed natural. The current tried to push her away from the structure, but she increased her kick and fought her way to her destination. She might be weightless, but her armor still had plenty of inertia, and it took effort to move her limbs against the resistance of the water.

Once she neared the scaffolding, she saw that it was a fallen tower partly draped atop the airlock. Perhaps the tower had once held a navigation light to help the submarine find its berth, but there was no light shining now, and the structure was crumpled, lying across the airlock like an exhausted animal. Sula tilted her body to look up with the floodlight and saw buoys nesting in corners of the structure or straining against fouled cables. She flashed her light to the capsules in their sleeves, the buoys and cables reaching upward. Hand over hand, she pulled herself along the fallen structure, took hold of one of the buoy cables, and pulled. Weightless despite her armor, she was unable to exert any proper force. Panting, she hooked one leg over the beam to anchor herself and began pulling the buoy's cable.

It came down easily. When she was able to get her hands on it, she found it the size of a large watermelon and just about as easy to wrestle. It took her several tries, but she managed to pass it under herself and the beam and let it fly free. The buoy rocketed away, the cable scraping against the fallen beam as it unspooled.

She gasped out a laugh as the cable whirred away,

scraping against the beam, then devoted herself to catching her breath. Everything here was *work*.

"I've cleared one of the buoys," she gasped. "Let me know if it reaches the surface."

The answer came less than a minute later, just a few seconds after the cable stopped its race. "Buoy's on the surface, miss!"

"The buoy will be transmitting the distress signal now," Sula said. "People will know we're here." Which was meant to cheer up the refugees in the airlock, but Sula knew perfectly well that the emergency services on Sulawesi were overwhelmed and might be unable to rescue them even if they received the signal. Certainly, no aircraft could venture out into the ash storm.

The voice returned. "Macnamara says he's ready to come out. Should he bring any tools?"

Sula considered. "If he and Spence can find anything like crowbars, they should bring them."

"I'll tell them."

Sula waited, leg anchored to the beam, as she looked down at the capsule in its sleeve. It would probably pop out of the sleeve all right, but it still needed to clear the tower scaffold before it could rise to the surface.

She was working on solutions to the problem when the planet gave a sudden leap, and she pivoted helplessly around the beam as it spun out from under her . . . and now she was inverted and drifting and surrounded by turbid darkness, and she might be turning slow circles in the murk, but she couldn't be sure. The shock had thrown up all the ash and mud and surrounded her with an opaque wall. She could barely see the light on her wrist. Her rank-smelling hair had fallen in her face.

"Are you people all right?" she called, her voice bright and sharp in the confined space of her helmet. She thought she sounded panicked and she hoped the others didn't agree.

The answer came right away. "We are just a little shaken, miss. Your man is in the airlock."

"Tell him not to come out just yet. The shock kicked the silt loose and he won't be able to see anything."

"We'll tell him, miss."

The brief dialog had calmed her, and she realized the current was pulling her away from the structure. She didn't know where in the cloud it was, and feared that if she let the current take her, she might not be able to find it again. Best, she thought, to decrease her buoyancy and sink to the bottom, where she could wait until the turbidity settled.

Numbers flickered greenly on the head-up display. Sula held her left wrist right up to the faceplate and could barely make out the controls—she paged through menus till she found the controls for buoyancy, and increased her weight until she settled face-first on the bottom, gentle as a feather on the black volcanic sand. She spat a strand of hair out of her mouth.

Sula threw up another huge cloud of sludge as she struggled to her feet, and she leaned slightly into the current and waited for the black sleet to settle. In the absolute darkness, she could see a reflection of her own face in the faceplate in front of her, and her heart froze. Caro Sula hung before her eyes in the black, cold water, the water where now she dwelled since her best friend had put her there.

Sula closed her eyes, but that only made it worse. Now she could imagine Caro's pale gold hair drifting in the darkness, the cold hands reaching for her. She smothered a scream. The impulse to bolt for the surface was overwhelming.

It's not real, she thought, and opened her eyes. She looked up into a corner of the faceplate, away from the pale face that stared at her from a few fingerbreadths away. Her heart was racing, her breath frantic. She fought the panic, tried to get her breathing under control.

Macnamara, she realized, was waiting in the trunk airlock. If he came out, he might be able to find her and help her. She triggered the underwater speakers.

"Macnamara," she panted. "Come out!"

She was answered by a burst of sound as chaotic as

the ash that swirled around her. She realized she was farther away from the structure than she thought, and for a moment, another surge of panic nearly submerged her. She increased volume and repeated the instructions to Macnamara.

"Hang on to the structure!" she added. "You don't want to get lost!"

Lost like me, she thought. *Lost in Caro Sula's dead domain.*

She waited, alone on the bottom, and watched the ash as it crawled in little streams across the corner of her faceplate. Her legs ached with the effort of maintaining her stance against the current. After some minutes, she realized that her lights were penetrating deeper into the murk.

"Macnamara," she called. "If you're out of the airlock, please shine your light left to right."

There was a buzzing reply. "Yes, my lady." At least that's what she decided she'd heard.

Sula turned in a slow circle, kicking up more clouds of silt and seeing nothing. It occurred to her that she was in the absolute worst place to see anything, since the silt and ash was drifting down and the turbidity would be more severe near the bottom. She needed to get away. She needed to give herself permission to fly.

"Keep flashing your light!" Sula said. She took hold

of the joystick and jetted off the bottom with her impellers. Her hardsuit still had negative buoyancy and the impellers brought her up slowly, her jets leaving behind yet another cloud of silt. She rose until she could see the beam from her helmet reaching out some distance into the darkness, then turned off all her lights and slowly turned in circles, her eyes straining into the darkness. Her heart lifted as she thought she saw a distant orange glow, a flash and then gone.

She wasn't alone anymore, alone in Caro's watery grave.

"Make a big circle with your light," she called, and the far-off orange light returned, tracking a crescent-shaped path—Sula assumed the rest of the circle was pointed in a different direction. She fired the impellers and arrowed toward the signal, and her mind eased as the beam brightened and turned into a full circle. She found Macnamara clinging to the outside of the trunk airlock, his right arm circling like mad, and Spence's head just poking out of the airlock door.

Sula draped her arms around Macnamara's neck and hung on, indescribable relief warm and bright in her mind. "My lady?" Macnamara said.

"Hang on to me," Sula said. "I'm too heavy." Macnamara held her while she neutralized her buoyancy, then she turned to the escape pod.

"I'll hover just above the pod," she said, "and when it pops up, I'll kick it away from the airlock. You two anchor yourselves up on the wreckage of the tower and shove it clear when it gets in range."

The other two tilted back to view the fallen tower, just visible above them in the murk.

"My lady?" Spence said. "The pod just climbs up the cable, yes?"

"That's right."

"Why don't we just tail onto the cable, pull it away from the wreckage, and keep it clear? The pod should go right up the line."

Sula considered this. "Well," she breathed. "I guess all I needed was to ask the engineer."

Sula told the survivors inside the airlock to get in the escape pod with the deployed buoy—it would be crowded, but they could be reasonably sure of getting away. "Once you're ready, bang on the pod three times, wait half a minute, then launch."

"We understand, miss."

Sula and the others maneuvered to the cable, then positioned themselves in a line along it, roughly at the level of the crumpled tower, after which there was nothing to do but wait. Sula watched the head-up display and felt a distant tugging on the cable as the buoy bobbed overhead. Her suit's heating unit had come on, warming her socks and soggy uniform trousers, and the suit was filled with a wet-dog smell.

Caro's presence seemed to have faded now that she was free of the muck. She breathed easier.

Three distinct clunks sounded out, the signal. "Let's pull, then," Sula said, wrapped both arms around the cable, and triggered the impellers. Spence's boots banged on her helmet as the three dragged the cable away in slightly different directions, and Sula snarled, not because she was angry at Spence but because she hated clumsiness.

The cable offered no resistance, but she could feel small shocks transmitted up the taut cable that indicated continued volcanic activity. Sula directed her helmet light down the cable to the escape pod and waited.

Long seconds ticked by, and Sula began to wonder if the pod was jammed in its sleeve. Then there was a loud clank as invisible clamps were withdrawn, and the pod bounced like a jack-in-the-box out of its sleeve, then started bobbing along its cable at a more measured pace. The pod's flashing emergency lights painted the scene red. Sula felt the cable jerk in her arms, and Spence's boots banged Sula's helmet again.

The three divers had drawn the cable out at an angle more horizontal than Sula would have liked, but the pod moved along the cable with calm assurance. Macnamara, below Sula, let go of the cable as the pod reached him, and the release of tension bobbed Sula upward and caused a momentary flash of alarm. She had to move her feet out of the way so that she could peer down to see the pod as it rose toward her. She let go of the cable to get out of the pod's way, and as it rose past her, Sula looked through the pod's window to see a terrified Anna Spendlove in the dim emergency lights, her eyes staring, face drained of color, hair hanging limp. *You look like hell,* Sula thought with satisfaction, and tilted her body to watch the pod as it rose.

It didn't leap for the surface as had the buoy, so Sula assumed there was a mechanism that kept it rising at a more measured pace. Because there was nothing else to do, Sula followed the pod upward, one armored hand grazing the cable to keep herself oriented.

The climb to the surface took only a few minutes, rising into the face of the black snow raining down from the surface. Outside the range of her lights and the red flashers, the darkness was total. To her surprise, on the final few seconds of the journey, the pod vanished into blackness, as if swallowed by a magician's cloak, and then she rose into the darkness herself and felt objects bumping and clattering against her helmet. It wasn't until she broke the surface and saw the emergency flashers and her helmet light on the surface of the water that she realized she was floating in a sea of pumice deep enough to reach her waist. The larger pumice stones were light enough to float, but they were raining down alongside smaller, denser ash that sank to the bottom. The weight of the pumice had calmed the sea, which was almost flat, rising only to low, broad waves that barely lifted her, only to settle her gently down again.

Pumice clattered on her helmet, pouring down in a steady stone shower. For the most part, the stones were small and light, but in her helmet flood she saw some larger than her fist floating nearby, and she didn't relish the thought of one of those cracking down out of the sky and landing on her faceplate.

Tropical heat pulsed through her helmet. Sula felt sweat dotting her forehead and hoped her suit's cooling units would kick in soon.

Macnamara and Spence came to the surface together a short distance away. The planes of their faces were turned bloodred by the scarlet flashers. Spence winced as clinkers bounced off her helmet, raised a hand protectively above her head.

The escape capsule bobbed above them, the buoy atop it leaning like a cocked dunce cap. There didn't seem to be a way to communicate with the survivors inside, and from the surface Sula couldn't look into the window to communicate with the occupants. They were stuck in the pod till help arrived.

The world was completely dark. Not a single star shone, and no light glowed on the horizon to indicate the presence of Tinombala on the shore. Sula panned her helmet light left and right, and saw a shadow on the water, one of the microwave receivers for the rectenna field, its great petals shadowing the water. The yellow hazard light that should have marked it, and all the other receivers, had either been shattered by falling stone or buried in rubble.

"Let's get under cover!" Sula told the others, and reinforced the suggestion with a gesture. She triggered the impellers and soon was plowing slowly through the sea of stones like a bluff-bowed ship. The rattling of stones on her helmet ceased, and she turned over to see one of the receiver dish's enormous petals cantilevered over her.

Macnamara and Spence surged up alongside her, pushing little bow waves. Even through the suit helmets, Sula could hear the clacking and clanging of the stones raining down on the receiver dish.

"I'm not sure I like this," Spence said. The distorted words grated from her underwater speakers, and Sula could feel a vibration in her hardsuit as the sound waves pulsed against it. "Those rocks are adding a lot of weight to the receiver dish. The whole thing could tip over without warning."

"We'll stay near the edge," Sula said. She was already paging through the menus on her control panel, found the communication menu, and turned on her radio antenna. To her surprise, she saw that she was receiving a strong signal.

She called Lieutenant-Captain Parku, her executive officer in the dockyard.

"My lady? Where are you?" His well-controlled Torminel tones betrayed neither surprise nor anxiety.

"Floating in the sea, in Tomini Bay off Sulawesi, with three Fleet personnel and a group of civilian survivors. There should be an emergency beacon marking our location. I'd be obliged if you could send a boat to pick us up."

This time Parku couldn't disguise his surprise. "You're in the *ocean*?" he blared.

"I'm in an armored diving suit and in no immediate danger, but I'd still like you to get a boat here. The civilians are probably in some distress. A couple hours ago, I saw a rescue boat patrolling offshore; perhaps you can contact it."

"I'll call Lieutenant-Captain Koridun. She's in charge of the whole rescue effort, she should know who to notify."

"Koridun has enough to do," Sula said firmly. "You can manage it from there, I'm sure."

Parku succeeded in suppressing any surprise or annoyance. "Of course, my lady. Stand by."

Sula waited for a few moments, rising and falling in the easy waves, and listened to the hiss and plash of the pumice raining down. Parku's melodious voice returned.

"My lady, I've contacted the rescue patrol. They're receiving your signal and are heading for your location."

"Thank you, Lord Koz. Can you give me a report?"

"It's the largest volcanic explosion in thousands of years, my lady. They heard the explosion as far as Sydney."

"Any problems at the skyhook terminal?"

"We have robots going up and down the cables, and so far, there's no report of any damage."

"Any estimate of casualties?"

"It's a little early for that," said Parku. "Tsunamis aren't a good sign, though."

"No, they're not.

"Thank you, Parku. If I need you again, I'll call."

"Yes, my lady. Thank you."

Grinding and rattling sounded from overhead as a shoal of ash shifted again. Spence gave Sula an imploring look. "My lady? Maybe we should move?"

"Agreed." Impellers drew them away from shelter, a blunt arrow plowing through the stony sea, and falling pumice rattled on their helmets again. Sula approached the bobbing escape pod, but the red flashing lights blinded her, and though she tried to make reassuring gestures in the direction of the window, she had no idea whether anyone saw or understood her.

"My lady!" Macnamara's hand touched her shoulder, spun her around. "Look!"

Coming toward them, white-hulled, brilliantly lit, searchlights probing the water ahead, was the rescue cutter.

Twenty minutes later, Sula was out of the armored suit and sat in the cabin of the rescue boat as she breathed pure oxygen through a mask and watched a crane hoist the escape pod onto the after deck. Clinkers rattled continually down, banging on the overhead and clanging off the windows, and half the Naxid crew was assigned to broom duty, sweeping the stuff overboard before it overbalanced the boat.

There was a clang as the escape pod opened, and its occupants spilled out over the deck like falling sacks of sand. Some were stained by vomit, so it appeared that even the gentle motion of the bay was too much for at least one passenger.

Anna Spendlove came out stained and wild-eyed, vomit dripping from her lap, her hair in limp strands over her face. Her wrists were still handcuffed, and one of the

Naxid crew had to steady her to keep her from falling on her face.

Sula smiled to herself. She thought that perhaps Spendlove was in just about the right frame of mind for an extended interrogation.

But first, she thought, she herself could use a wash. She asked the Naxid captain if there were a shower available, and the captain had one of the petty officers take her belowdecks and show her the facilities. The shower was meant for Naxids, and so Sula had to squat to avoid hitting her head. There was no shampoo, and the soap was meant to keep beaded scales glossy, but at least she was able to wash off the dust and grime. She brushed her uniform blouse and trousers, and returned to the deck feeling more like an officer than a refugee.

Spendlove, trussed and vomit-stained, was in no condition to resist. She said that she'd been recruited for the impersonation on Zanshaa by a young Torminel who'd called himself "Colti," though he frankly admitted the name was an alias. He was well dressed, with an aristocratic air and High City accent, and Spendlove—who had devoted her life to studying and impersonating people she wasn't—thought the posh manner genuine.

He's simply offered too much money to resist. "And besides," Spendlove added, "he said you were a murderer."

True enough, Sula thought, *as far as that goes.*

"Did he mention who I'm supposed to have killed?" she asked.

"No," Spendlove said. "And I didn't want to know."

"Do you have any idea who Colti might actually be?"

Spendlove shook her head. "I don't know every Peer on Zanshaa. And for that matter, I don't know whether or not he was a Peer, or whether he just had a Peer's access to money."

"Was he working on behalf of someone else, or was this his own project?"

"He didn't mention anyone else. He seemed very committed, so if he wasn't actually in charge, he was a very enthusiastic participant."

Sula asked if Colti was on Terra.

"I don't think so. He turned me over to someone else, a female Torminel who called herself Sori. Also posh, also young. I've only met her a couple times."

"What did she wear?"

Spendlove gave the question some thought. "Casual clothes—shorts and short-sleeve shirts so she wouldn't overheat. Top of the line, though. Roote & Orghoder is expensive."

"Where did you meet?"

"On the ring, shortly after I arrived. And then once in Rome, a little over a month ago."

"Could you identify her or Colti?"

"If I met them in person. If I was asked to identify from photographs, I couldn't be sure." She frowned. "Torminel are covered in fur. I have a hard time telling them apart."

"Any distinguishing characteristic you can recall?"

Spendlove passed a hand over her red-rimmed eyes. "Sori had very blue eyes. That's not common."

Cold triumph whispered quietly through Sula's blood. "No," she said, "it's not."

———————

Eleven hours later, on a morning dark with cloud and ashfall, the volcano was still in full eruption, but southwesterly winds had blown the lithic storm out to sea. Sula and her party were in a police van, with intact windows but otherwise identical to their last vehicle, following a road plow carving out a path to Tambu. Clearing the roads was a priority, since the falling ash would turn to concrete if it rained.

Spendlove had been left behind in the Tinombala jail. Sula didn't want her in Tambu, not until certain matters there were dealt with.

The plow and the police van climbed over Sulawesi's narrow spine. The tropical forest had been nearly shattered: limbs torn from trees, leaves stripped, treetops bowed down under tons of ash and rock. The air had an acid reek that burned the back of Sula's throat. Towns and villages were strewn with homes collapsed under ash or buried in drifts of pumice. Emergency vehicles were clustered near large public buildings, which seemed to have fared better.

Sulawesi's communications network was robust, and Sula experienced little difficulty in performing her researches. Fortunately, Peers were proud of their genealogies and made sure the information was widely available. It was easy to work out who Colti was, and of course Sori was obvious. And a look at the genealogy told her who Sula was supposed to have killed.

Macnamara and Spence slumped in the back seats, trying to sleep, while Sula thought long into the morning, planning what she had to do next.

The plow led Sula's party right to the elevator terminal and beneath the sweeping portico that so far had stood up well to so many extra tons of ash. Sula thanked the drivers of the van and the plow, and walked in to a scene of ongoing chaos.

Each refugee had staked out a piece of floor large enough for a sleeping mat or blanket, with a little extra room for a bundle of belongings. Children of all species were running over the giant concourse while parents did their best to organize or distract them. There were food smells, none of them appetizing, and the stench of urine warred with that of disinfectant.

Sula headed for the rear of the concourse, where she guessed she could find the administrative offices. She was back in uniform again, a Fleet fatigue overall in viridian green, with her firearm buckled to her belt. Macnamara and Spence followed with the baggage, which had been rescued from the wrecked police van in Tinombala.

Sula had released her other guard, the one who had met her at the waterfront the previous evening. "There are more important jobs for you than guarding me," she'd told him, and he'd seemed relieved to hear it.

And of course, she didn't want him around for what she planned to do.

She passed the lounge where she'd met Goojie just a few days before and saw it was filled with refugees, some of whom were lucky enough to be able to sleep on plush sofas. She encountered Lieutenant-Captain Koridun on the way to the lifts to the offices, and Koridun rushed to her.

"Captain Sula! Where have you been? We expected you last night!" She braced and waited for the reply.

"I was in Tinombala. I was called there to deal with a problem at the Power Authority—you didn't get the message?"

Koridun seemed startled. "No, my lady. I—"

"It doesn't matter. By the time I got there, all the people I needed to talk to had evacuated, and the eruption trapped me there till now."

Koridun seemed eager to help. "If you'll give me their names, I'll put you in contact—"

"It doesn't matter now. Can you show me a place to put my gear, and give me a report?"

"Of course, my lady!"

She gave a look to Spence and Macnamara. "I sent you two constables," she said. "Are they with you?"

"One was injured in Tinombala and is in the clinic there. I sent the other back to his unit—I hardly think anyone's going to try to kill me in the middle of this mess."

Koridun reserved judgment on this last and took Sula to the manager's suite on the top floor of the giant building, and put Sula and her bags in the manager's private study. She looked at Spence and Macnamara. "The enlisted are bunking in Departure Lounge One."

"They'll stay with me," Sula said. Koridun made no comment but instead took Sula into the manager's office, where she met the manager herself, a Daimong engineer in coveralls and heavy boots, with her helmet resting on her desktop. The view from the office was impressive, a glass wall looking out over a bay filled with wrecked, half-sunken boats and floating islands of pumice. The buildings on the slopes below all seemed to have suffered damage, but the elevator terminal survived well, glass wall and all.

"It was designed for this, my lady," the manager said. "The area is subject to volcanism and earthquake, and the architects overbuilt everything."

"Lucky for us," Sula said.

Koridun gave her report quickly and without hesitation—not surprising, since she was an ambitious officer, well organized, and had been granted an extra night to practice her delivery.

Neither the elevator cables nor the building had suffered significant damage. Employees had been set to work aiding the refugees, and Fleet personnel were keeping order and helping the local police.

As for the eruption, it was the largest on Terra in several thousand years. Particulates and sulfuric acid had been hurled nearly to the border of space and would remain in the atmosphere for years, sealing out the sunshine. There would be severe danger of crop failure, and Lord Governor Ngeni had appealed to the Convocation for emergency food supplies to be sent at once. He had also mobilized relief workers from all over the planet, but they couldn't land any closer than South Sulawesi until the eruption died away. So, the workers and supplies would jam ports far to the south and have to head for

Tambu on roads and rail lines covered with deep drifts of ash.

"My compliments, Captain Koridun," Sula said. "Very concise. You've done well."

Koridun practically glittered with pride. "Thank you, Lady Sula."

Sula asked if there was anything she could do in regard to readying more aid from the dockyards, but Koridun said that she and Parku between them had done everything possible. Plenty of assistance, food, and aid could come down the elevators as soon as it was safe to bring it all down.

In the meantime, all they had to do was endure.

"I'll just stand by here, then," Sula said. "You've been doing well, and I don't want to interrupt if I'm not needed. If I have a suggestion, I'll offer it, but otherwise it's your show; you may as well continue."

So, for the next few hours Sula watched Koridun at her job, coordinating her efforts with the manager of the elevator complex, and through the communications net with the local lady governor, the lord mayor, the lord police commissioner, and Parku up on the ring. All day, small shocks rattled the items on her desk. The plows were clearing the streets, and trapped refugees were being brought aid or being brought to where aid waited for them.

As the afternoon waned, even the active, ever-buoyant Koridun began to show signs of fatigue, and Sula recollected that she'd been engaged in this nonstop for more than a day. So, she sent Koridun for some rest and raw meat, if she could find any of the latter, and took command of the Fleet effort herself.

When she had a moment to herself, she filed charges against the crew of the Power Authority submarine for cowardice and dereliction of duty. *I'll avalanche them,* she thought.

Koridun returned after midnight, and Sula retired with Macnamara and Spence to the manager's study, with its screens showing views of the ring and the stars. The room was scented with sandalwood. Sula placed Spence right across the door, to foil the next assassin, and then lay on the leather cushions of a sofa and fell instantly to sleep.

Sula woke to the largest single sound she'd ever heard, her fingers clutching at the frame of the couch to keep her from being thrown out as a vast shock seemed to snap the tower like a whip. From somewhere there was a cry, and then a crash as something tipped over.

The building groaned as it settled. Sula stuck her feet in her boots, tightened her Fleet coverall, and charged out to the manager's office, leaping over Spence's startled form.

Through the glass wall—not broken—she could see that it wasn't yet dawn. Koridun and the Daimong manager were seated at their desks, staring at each other.

"Ground wave coming," Sula predicted, and then the building rocked again. Its metal skeleton keened for a long, desperate moment, and then the sound went away, replaced by a series of smaller shocks that set Sula's head aspin.

Sula contacted Parku, on the assumption that observatories on the ring would have a much better idea of what was going on than local authorities. He confirmed that there had been another large explosion on Karangetang, probably the largest so far, but that was all he knew.

"Tell everyone on the streets to get under cover," Sula told Koridun. "There may be van-sized chunks of basalt coming down."

Basalt boulders didn't rain on Tambu, but practically everything else did—blocks of stone the size of fists, razor-edged shards of glass, ash, pumice finer than sand. The westerly wind that had earlier blown the ejecta away was overwhelmed, or perhaps silenced by the great shock wave, because all the debris came down freely. There was nothing to do but watch it fall and hear the constant rattle of stones piling up on the roof. The smell of ash penetrated the room despite its controlled climate.

There was no dawn, only a black sky pouring debris.

At midmorning, there was an emergency call. "Building collapse—some kind of public school annex that was being used to house refugees," Koridun reported. "There's a call for transport to evacuate the survivors, and ambulances for casualties."

This was more or less what Sula had been waiting for. She composed her face into a thoughtful expression. "Let's go, then. But we're going to need a plow to carve a path for us."

Koridun gave her a surprised look. "You want to go yourself?"

"I want us both to go," Sula said. "We need to evaluate the rescue efforts firsthand. And we should inspect as much as we can so that we can transmit proper reports to the ring and to Lord Governor Ngeni and other officials here on Terra." Sula smiled. "It's my proactive policy."

The governor's name, and with it the possibility that her own name might be mentioned favorably in a report, was more than enough to galvanize Koridun's ambition. She arranged to borrow a plow from the local authority, and a vehicle for themselves. Sula and the party were equipped with helmets, cuirasses, and flashlights.

The plow was waiting when they came out into the tropical heat beneath the portico, got into a six-wheeled vehicle meant for primitive or nonexistent roads, and followed the plow out into the hard black rain. Rocks began banging off the six-wheeler's roof the second they left the shelter of the portico.

Black ash, black roads, black crumpled buildings. The beams of the headlights were swallowed up by darkness, and falling rocks carved divots out of the windscreen. There was so much ejecta on the roads that there was really no place to put it: the plow carved only a narrow strip between tall shoals of debris.

Claustrophobia climbed into the passenger compartment. Macnamara's fists clenched on the controls.

The fallen school annex was less than ten minutes away, even at the reduced speed of the convoy. Emergency vehicles were already clustered around the building, lights flashing off the crumbling walls. The building was large and situated on a tongue of land between ravines. The plow performed a wide sweep through the flat area in front of the building, carving out as large a debris-free zone as possible, and following it Sula saw a small shed-like outbuilding on a corner of the property. Macnamara drew up as close to the rescue effort as he could, while the plow continued to clear as much of the area as possible.

Sula rolled up her door and jumped out of the vehicle, only to be greeted by a bang on her helmet as a lava bomb struck and bounded off. The acid stench of the ash clawed at the back of her throat. Sula saw refugees clustered near a door, their possessions on their heads, and stepped through the crowd and the rattling stone into the building, her flashlight darting over the area.

The annex was a broad, flat-roofed structure, with offices on one end and a warehouse on the other, and only the warehouse part had collapsed. There had been plenty of warning that the roof was giving way, and there were no casualties save for the crushed boxes of athletic equipment stored there. The remaining roofbeams groaned ominously, and Sula looked up and felt a cold warning hand brush her spine. Whoever had called for the evacuation hadn't been wrong.

The first of the buses came up, and refugees were packed aboard with the clearly impossible instruction to keep away from the windows, some of which had already shattered. More buses arrived, and more refugees made the dash from their shelter. The emergency personnel on hand were a mixture of Fleet security, local police, and aid workers, and they all acted with practiced efficiency. They'd been evacuating people all day.

Finally, the last refugee was helped aboard the final bus, and the convoy began to leave, plows clearing the way. Sula complimented the Naxid in charge of the relief party, and then she and her group returned to their vehicle, cleared ash from the windscreen, and piled aboard. Macnamara took the controls.

"Wait," Sula said. "Does anyone remember that other building?"

"My lady?" Koridun said. She was panting behind her faceplate and suffering in the tropical heat, her fur blackened with streaks of ash. Her cooling units weren't keeping up with the climate.

Sula pointed. "Back there. We should check. There could be refugee families in there."

Macnamara swung the vehicle around and ground over cinders until the outbuilding appeared in the lights. The structure hadn't collapsed, probably because the pitched shed roof tipped debris into the ravine just beyond. "Come on," Sula said, rolled up the door, and jumped out of the vehicle. A block of lava landed close by and exploded, sending out shrapnel that stung Sula's legs. Beyond where the plow had swept the area clear, the ejecta came nearly to her waist, and she had to climb over the stuff to get to the door. She banged on the door, heard no response, tried the handle, and found that it opened.

Ash spilled into the room as Sula half-slid into the shed. Stones rattled off the metal roof overhead. There was a musty chemical scent in the room, and large barrels of lubricant and paint, volatile materials probably unwelcome in the larger building.

No refugees, which Sula had more or less assumed.

Koridun slid into the building next, followed by

Spence and Macnamara. They clustered near the door, prepared to head back to the vehicle, but Sula seized the moment by raising her faceplate and looking at Koridun. Koridun raised her own faceplate.

"Lady Sula?"

"I wanted to tell you again how impressed I am with you. It's been a difficult situation and you've done very well."

Koridun's blue eyes glowed with pride. "Thank you, my lady."

Sula eased the strap on her sidearm's holster. "But there's something we should talk about," she said, "and that's your Aunt Trani."

There was a moment of silence, and then the glow in Koridun's blue eyes turned glacial. "You killed her," she said.

"I didn't."

"Your army did. You don't expect me to believe that happened without your permission."

Well, no, Sula thought, *I don't.*

A look at Koridun's family tree had easily uncovered the relationship with the obscure Peer clan of the Creels, one of which had been lucky enough to marry a Koridun two generations back. Trani Creel, assassinated a few days after being appointed governor of Zanshaa, had been Koridun's aunt.

Spence and Macnamara exchanged glances and sidled away from Koridun. Both were reaching for their sidearms.

"Aunt Trani was a *wonderful* person!" Koridun said. Her diction was slipping, and the words hissed through her fangs. "My brother and I were raised with her after my mother went to the hospital—she was like a big sister! She told us stories! She sang us to sleep at night! We loved her, and *you killed her!*"

You might have noticed she was an idiot, Sula thought.

Not that she'd been very bright herself. If she'd only paid better attention to Koridun's service record, she would have been suspicious the instant she'd learned that Koridun had volunteered for service on Terra.

Nobody volunteered for Terra. It was a one-way ticket to oblivion. Anyone volunteering for Terra clearly had an agenda other than career advancement.

Koridun raised a pointing finger. "You'll pay for it! We won't rest until you do!"

That's what I'm afraid of, Sula thought. She cleared ash from her throat, spat, and turned back to Koridun. "You should know that Costanza Vole—or Anna Spendlove, or Tamlin Sage, whatever name you prefer—has been arrested and is cooperating with police. She's identified you as a member of the plot to discredit me."

Koridun panted for breath. Stones rattled on the roof.

Her eyes darted from Sula to the others and back, and it was clear she realized acutely that she was the only person in the shed without a firearm. "I don't know anyone by those names," she said.

"Your brother's behind this, isn't he?" Sula said. "He's spending an absurd amount on this ridiculous scheme."

He was young, Sula knew, and the previous Lord Koridun had skipped two generations of his own descendants in order to bestow the title on his great-grandson. The generations he'd skipped had been renowned for debauchery, mental instability, and violence extreme even for Torminel—the hospital to which Koridun's mother had been sent was for lunatics—and the late lord had probably hoped that his great-grandson would prove more sober and sensible than his parents.

He'd been overly optimistic. Koridun's brother, masterminding this interplanetary revenge plot, was just as crazy as the others.

"We *hate* you!" Koridun's fangs flared white in the dark room.

"Lady Tari," Sula told Koridun, "your only chance is to cooperate. You've got to name everyone connected with this and—"

Koridun *squalled,* a nerve-splintering shriek designed to paralyze the carnivore Torminel's prey, and then she charged. Her fur stood erect, making her seem like a gi-

ant gray-black demon, and her face was completely ob-
scured save for her bared fangs and her furious blue eyes.

Sula had been half-prepared for something like this.
The shed was too small to avoid Koridun entirely, but
Sula stepped and pivoted out of the way, bracing against
the impact. Koridun's fangs flashed past Sula's face, and
her armored cuirass cracked against Sula's. The two re-
bounded from one another, Sula taking another step
back, Koridun going into a stack of barrels. She flung herself around and charged again, but by now, Sula's pistol had had time to clear the holster, and she shot Koridun through the open faceplate of her helmet. Koridun
flailed and fell, and Sula, with careful deliberation, shot
her again.

There was a long moment when time seemed sus-
pended, and Sula's heart pounded louder than the report
of her pistol, louder than the crash of volcanic debris
on the roof. Macnamara and Spence had their pistols
out, and they were staring at Koridun's body in wild
astonishment.

"Fuck," Spence breathed. "Creeping fucking fuck!"

Sula tried to get her heart and breathing under control.
Her arm was still outthrust, the pistol shaking to the
tsunami of adrenaline that rocked her body. She engaged
her pistol's safety and returned it to the holster, and ab-
sently thought to herself she'd have to toss the gun some-

where it wouldn't be found. She stepped to the body and bent over it. The tang of propellant flavored the air.

"We've got to get the breastplate off," she said. "I'm going to need her jacket."

"My lady?" Macnamara said.

"Then we toss the body into the ravine," Sula said. Her hands unclamped the cuirass on the right side.

"I'm a *constable*," Macnamara said in a reasonable tone. "Shawna and I can witness that she attacked you, and that it was self-defense."

Sula straightened and looked at him. "If word gets to Lord Koridun that I've shot his sister, he'll send a hundred more assassins after me. I've got to make it look as if his sister died in an accident."

Which was plausible, she hoped, but not the real reason. If word of the Koridun conspiracy got out, the Legion of Diligence was almost certain to take charge of the investigation. And while those merciless enforcers of the Praxis could be counted on to put an end to Lord Koridun and any offending members of his family—plus the usual gang of innocents caught up in the investigation—they might also get it into their stubborn, inflexible heads to investigate the death of Lady Governor Trani Creel, and Sula couldn't afford that.

No, she had other ways to deal with Lord Koridun and his clan.

Macnamara looked as if he was considering objecting to her argument, but decided against it. "Very well, my lady," he said. His face was sulky.

If a subordinate's bad mood was the worst thing that came out of this situation, Sula reckoned she could survive it. She and Macnamara stripped off the cuirass, then the uniform vest Koridun wore underneath it. As Sula's uniform tunic held Sula's communication gear and sleeve display, Koridun's vest also contained hardware that kept her in touch with the world, and which also located her in space. If the vest wasn't pulled off the corpse, the body could be located.

After the vest was removed, Sula and Macnamara wrestled the body up the drift of clinkers spilling through the door, then got it around the building and pitched it into the ravine just below the shed. Debris falling off the shed roof would bury it quickly, and if the ejecta kept coming down, Koridun would be buried under tons of rock that could stand for centuries. No one would have a reason to excavate that ravine, and perhaps they'd have every reason to build over it.

Sula threw Koridun's cuirass after the body, and carrying the vest, she and the others returned to their vehicle, swept debris off the windscreen, and began the return journey. Macnamara drove in stony silence, a little muscle twitching his jaw. Spence said nothing and seemed to be in shock.

It had been a very full twenty-four hours, certainly.

They caught up to the slower-moving convoy and soon after that turned aside to bring the six-wheeler beneath the swooping portico of the great elevator building. Within minutes, Sula was back in her quarters, and she took out Koridun's vest and turned off all its electronics. Any record of Koridun's movements would show that she had returned to her own headquarters.

She'd chop up the vest later and dispose of what remained.

After a shower, Sula was back in the manager's operations room, standing before the great clear window and looking out at the black storm that fell indifferently on the living and on the dead. She felt it was burying the Terra of her dreams, the magical place that had filled the fantasies of a young girl on Spannan.

That place, if it had existed at all, had died long before. A few monuments remained, as tortured and twisted by time as the Sphendone in Constantinople, but the civilizations that produced them had vanished, and the monuments survived only out of context, cenotaphs placed over the dust of the people that had built them. What remained was a sad, third-rate imitation of an imperial culture that was itself a patchwork jigsawed into place by half a dozen species surviving precariously under the despotic rule of vainglorious Shaa blockheads. The dreams of Terrans were no longer Terran but the dreams imposed by the Shaa and the culture of Zanshaa High City—and neither, she had learned, were worth anyone's dreams.

Her dreams, it seemed, were mortal. Mortal as Byzantium, or the empire of the Persians, or the city that was even now being buried under millions of tons of debris.

Everything dies, she thought as she looked out at the falling stone. *Nothing matters.*

In her present mood, she found the thoughts comforting.

———————

A little less than a month later, she was back in her quarters on the ring, preparing to receive Aram, Lord Tacorian in the paneled dining room of her suite. The president and founder of the Manado Company would be her guest for luncheon.

It would be the first time she'd served anyone off her new porcelain.

It hadn't been difficult to get Lord Tacorian to meet her. All she had to do was hint that she was ready to sign the contract permitting *Manado* free use of the Fleet dockyard.

Back on Terra, the eruption of Karangetang had come

to an end when the volcanic peak had collapsed into the empty magma chamber, and the waters of the Celebes Sea closed over the remains. The island had ceased to exist.

So had the city of Manado, which had been obliterated by a pyroclastic flow that had run across the surface of the strait, after which the ruins were entombed in ejecta deep enough to bury a three-story building. Because the city had been evacuated, only a few hundred lives were estimated to have been lost, far less than the eighty thousand estimated to have been killed when a series of tsunamis struck the east coast of Borneo. There had been more warning in the Philippines, and only a few thousand had died there.

Most of Tambu had received enough ashfall to creep halfway up second-floor windows. Some of the lower parts of the city were completely buried. There was too much to remove; a new city would have to be built atop the old, with the old city becoming cellars and foundations.

The skyhook cables had suffered only minor damage during the eruption, easily repaired by robots, and were now carrying a substantial amount of traffic as vast amounts of food, other supplies, and relief workers were being carried down to Sulawesi.

Koridun, along with thousands of others, was safely

buried under tons of debris. On the theory that she'd gone out to supervise some kind of rescue effort and been overcome by ejecta or crushed by a collapsing building, a search for her was under way through the improvised morgues that had been set up throughout Tambu, and Sula had to feign an interest in the results. She suspected that Koridun wouldn't be found for millions of years, not until the volcanic deposit in which she was buried eroded away under the slow, steady drip of geologic time.

Anna Spendlove had gone missing as well. The jail in Tinombala where she was being held had partially collapsed, and during the evacuation, she'd managed to slip away into the darkness and the stony rain. Sula presumed that if Spendlove had survived, she was trying as hard as possible not to look like Sula anymore. There was still a planetwide search for her, and there was every hope that she'd be spotted if she ever took the elevator to the ring in an attempt to flee Terra.

Sula hoped for Spendlove's sake that she wouldn't attempt to contact any of the people who had sponsored her visit to Terra. They had far more reason to kill than to help her.

Sula had done her part in the charade and written the late Lieutenant-Captain Koridun a commendation, and put her in for a medal for her work during the eruption.

She'd also written to her brother, Lord Koridun, complimenting her actions and assuring him that she was leaving no stone unturned in her search for her missing officer. Unspoken was the truth that there were far too many stones to turn them all.

In the meantime, she had sent a message to a friend, Julian Bakshi. Julian was a leader of the hard core of fighters who had spearheaded Sula's army during the rebellion, a murderous elite that had been drawn mainly from the ranks of the underworld. Julian had been one of those who had arranged for Trani Creel to meet her end, and no doubt he would be *very* interested in Lord Koridun's attempts to avenge her.

In fact, Sula now supposed that the Koridun clan would suffer more tragedies in the coming year, Lord Koridun's death chief among them.

Sula's message would be hand-delivered by Spence, who was now en route to the capital. Sula had considered Macnamara for the job, but Macnamara had never approved of Sula's making use of gangsters, and he hadn't known Sula's part in the Lady Governor's death. Sula thought she really didn't want any more of Macnamara's disapproval and had sent Spence instead. Spence might or might not approve, but she wouldn't sulk about it.

And now Sula was back on the ring, surrounded by her own personnel and her own guards. And about to serve her guest on her own porcelain, the tulip-and-pomegran-ate pattern she'd bought in Cappadocia. While she waited, she filled the teapot and poured herself a cup that she sweetened with cane sugar syrup. The black ly-chee tea had a pleasant vanilla undertone that soothed her. She had finished half the cup before Macnamara an-nounced her guest.

Lord Tacorian was relatively young, a vigorous man still under forty Earth years, with wiry, wavy dark hair, large brown eyes, and a slightly off-center nose with a bump on the bridge. He wore a chocolate-brown suit of soft, lightweight wool over immaculate white ruffles. His walk, she thought, might best be described as a saunter.

A confident man, Sula thought. Despite the title that had given him his start, he and his company were largely self-made. When he spoke, it was with one of Terra's more obscure accents.

"Lady Sula."

"My lord. Will you take a seat?"

"Delighted. Thank you."

"May I offer wine? Some other beverage?"

Tacorian smiled. "If that's tea you're drinking, I'll have some."

Macnamara, acting as a server, poured tea, then col-lected the wine glasses and carried them away. Sula of-fered cheese huffers and smiled. "I hope the Manado

Company will survive the destruction of Manado itself."

"We're fairly decentralized, so yes. We were able to evacuate our personnel and their dependents to the ring before the explosion, and now most of them are back on Earth, employed in our other offices."

"And your interstellar ships will be in a position to take advantage of all the food aid shipments coming to Earth."

He offered an easy smile. "That's true. It's a shame to profit from such a tragedy, but we're in a good position, with so many other companies' ships destroyed in the war."

Macnamara appeared with a trolley and the luncheon prepared by Sula's Cree chef Turney: a salad, crepes stuffed with walnuts and the celebrated lamb jerky of Ereğli, and an artistic swirl of creamed krek-tuber. Complex odors wafted through the air. Macnamara refilled the teacups and bowed his way out.

Sula had told him not to interrupt the meal unless she called for him. The conversation was bound to upset someone of Macnamara's temperament, and Sula preferred not to provoke any more sulks.

"I wanted to talk to you personally, Lord Tacorian," Sula said. "About the contract to berth *Manado* in the Fleet dockyard. I spoke about it to Lord Peltrot, and I think we got off on the wrong foot somehow."

Tacorian tented his thick eyebrows. "Lord Peltrot *can* be brusque."

"He was brusque enough when I met him," Sula said. "And then, of course, he hired an assassin to kill me."

Tacorian halted a fork en route to his mouth, then lowered it. "You have evidence of this?" he asked.

"Let's say only that evidence exists," Sula said. This was a lie, but she thought it a convincing one, particularly to anyone burdened with a guilty conscience. "Now the question in my mind," she continued, "is whether as operations officer, Lord Peltrot needed the permission of the president or the board of directors to hire an assassin, or whether he did it on his own."

Tacorian dabbed his mouth with his napkin while he considered his answer. "I think you must already know the answer," he said, "otherwise you'd be talking to me through the bars of a cell."

"Lord Peltrot's hiring a murderer seems to be only one of his many bad decisions," Sula said. "He's a Daimong, and Daimongs can't change their expression—and as a result they don't pay a lot of attention to the fine details of the expression of others. It turns out he couldn't tell one blond Terran female from another—he gave his bribe to the wrong person, and then he tried to kill *me* for not following through."

Tacorian's brows formed a crease between them. "He

bribed the . . . the celebrated impersonator?"

Anna Spendlove's activities had become public when Lady Commissioner Bjorge had begun investigations of the companies that had bribed her. The material was sensational and would have created a media firestorm if the eruption of Karangetang hadn't displaced it in the world's attention.

"He gave her four percent of your company," Sula said. "No cash changed hands, so nothing ended up in Spendlove's phony bank account, and the police never found out about it. And since the stock is in my name, I suppose it's actually mine."

Tacorian seemed amused. "Some compensation for all you've been through, I suppose. Keep it with my compliments."

Sula took a deliberate sip of tea. "I'm willing to sign the *Manado* agreement, but only under certain conditions."

Tacorian spread his hands. "Lady Sula, you have the floor."

"First," Sula said, "Lord Peltrot has to go. He's created a culture of violence within the company, and sooner or later, his bad judgment may wreck everything. He could land you all in jail."

Lord Tacorian didn't seem deeply troubled by the idea.

"You can't just sack him, of course," Sula added.

"You'll need to leave him enough of an incentive not to wreck everything on his way out. He should probably retire with a pension and with stock options—but I'd be *very* disappointed if he ended up spectacularly rich."

"I think what you ask is possible," Tacorian said carefully.

"You could, of course, kill him. I wouldn't have a problem with that."

Tacorian chose to affect amusement. "I'm shocked at the suggestion."

"The second thing I'd like," Sula said, "is that I'd like my investment in your company doubled."

Tacorian narrowed his eyes. "I'm not sure a berth in the Fleet dockyard is worth all of that."

"Consider what's at stake." Sula leaned back in her chair and smiled. "How many habitable planets have you found, Lord Tacorian?"

Because Sula was looking for them, she saw a series of small tremors cross Lord Tacorian's face all in the space of less than a second, a reaction far more candid than the measured reply that followed.

"I can't imagine what you're thinking, Lady Sula."

"*Manado*'s been on a series of mysterious missions to the Kuiper Belt," Sula said. "Continuing a series of trips made by other craft since before the war, originally carried out by your partner Captain Patel. Your patron, Lord

Mogna, has vastly increased his investment in your company and arranged for a warship badly needed in the Fleet to be diverted to your use—I don't have the precise figures, but your company's material wealth has increased by something like ten thousand percent.

"*Manado*'s taking shuttles out, and those shuttles have to fly somewhere. You're bringing back samples for analysis. On the last trip, *Manado* took an ecologist and a mining engineer, which makes sense if you've found a habitable world that you intend to exploit."

"All this would also make sense if we found a rich asteroid," Tacorian pointed out.

"If it was an asteroid, why haven't you filed a claim on it? It's been years."

Lord Takorian chose a judicious silence.

"My lord," said Sula, "I've been *looking*. I've had telescopes and other detectors pointed at *Manado* since its departure, and we saw it *vanish*. Now, it might have cut its engines and powered down to reduce its heat signature, but why would it do such a thing? Why would it be hiding out there, and why on its return would it need the increased security of a Fleet dockyard? Plus, going black is very difficult for a ship the size of *Manado*, which is why we never tried it in the war and used decoys instead." She nodded. "Lastly, if you'd found a valuable asteroid or planetoid, you wouldn't need the vast increase in carrying capacity that Lord Mogna has provided for you. But you'll need all that if you want to transport immigrants and supplies to a new settlement." She tilted her head and looked at him. "The one question I can't manage to answer is why none of the earlier surveys found the wormhole."

Lord Tacorian took a long breath, then let it out. "The wormhole is in orbit around a planetoid. It must have been eclipsed when the earlier surveys were run and any associated electromagnetic phenomena put down to conditions on the planetoid."

"And your Captain Patel discovered it?"

"Indeed she did."

"So, what's on the other side?"

Tacorian took another breath. "A solar system with a perfect, habitable planet the size of Zanshaa. And a second cold, dry world that's barely habitable but with a climate that could be adjusted over time. All we'd need to do is decrease the surface albedo, then the glaciers would melt and the place could become quite cozy. It would take centuries, but we could make it a lovely world."

"And you need to keep your discovery secret until arrangements can be made in Zanshaa for your company to be primary contractor on the settlement, with Lord Mogna as patron."

"Lord Mogna's *already* patron of Devajjo. It's unlikely they'd give him a second world."

Sula nodded. "So, that's a reward to be dangled before some key politician or other. Or a second reward, if you count the colder world."

"There are three. Because we've found another wormhole in the system that leads to another system and another inhabitable world."

Sula tried to keep her mouth from dropping open. "It would be like the Hone Reach," she said. A series of habitable systems opening up one after the other, with Earth as the door. Any efforts at settlement would be based on Earth, and any trade with the newly settled worlds would have to pass through Sol's system.

From being a sad, provincial, dead-end world, Earth would become key to a bonanza.

"How long before you make the announcement?" Sula asked.

"At least two years. Maybe more. Things in Zanshaa..." Lord Tacorian waved a hand vaguely. "Things aren't yet in order."

Which meant, Sula thought, that not enough of the Lords Convocate had yet been bribed. These things took time: the project's secrecy meant that none of them could be told exactly what it was they were being bribed to *do*, because if the secret got out, factions among the

Convocates would start scrambling to harvest the worlds for themselves. Negotiations were bound to be a little on the delicate side.

Lord Tacorian shifted in his chair, then leaned forward and put his elbows on the table. "Let's do a little dickering," he said.

The end result of the conversation was that Sula would get her additional four percent in four years, after her term as governor of the dockyard was over. It would frankly be a reward for her cooperation in the interim, and Sula didn't have a problem with that. Lord Tacorian was willing to sign a document formalizing the arrangement.

Getting rid of Lord Peltrot Convil was going to be more difficult, since he was so entrenched in the company's business, but Tacorian assured her that it would happen. Sula was tempted to arrange to have him killed herself, but considered that after having killed one enemy on Earth, and having just entered a war of assassination against a prominent Peer clan on Zanshaa, she was involved in quite enough mayhem for the present and taking quite enough chances.

Lady Commissioner Bjorge was still investigating Goojie's murder, the misdeeds of Anna Spendlove, and any theoretical connection between the two—and might, if she was sufficiently thorough or lucky, find the actual sponsors of the crimes, which would take Lord Peltrot off the table without Sula having to raise a finger. Sula could only hope.

"One last request," Sula said finally, after all the arrangements had been completed. "May I ask that you name one of your new cities Ermina, after my cousin who was killed?"

"Of course," said Lord Tacorian with a smile. "I'd be very pleased to do it, my lady."

After which they had an agreeable lunch, during which Tacorian decided he'd take up Sula's offer of wine after all. So, a bottle was brought, and while Sula watched, Tacorian drank several glasses and toasted their new arrangement. He swayed just a little when he left.

Poor man, Sula thought, *he's had a bad shock. And lost a few hundred billion of the theoretical trillions of zeniths he'd possibly make someday if everything worked out.*

Sula returned to her office after the meeting with Tacorian and looked out of her little tower at the dockyard with its small ships, cranes, tangles of pipes, solar collectors, and robots performing routine maintenance, all brilliantly lit in the glare of Earth's sun. The ring, which from this perspective looked absolutely flat, seemed to stretch to infinity in either direction, like a highway into the heavens.

She couldn't see Earth. It was above her head, with the

mass of the ring in the way.

Earth, which was about to experience a rebirth. Enough money would fall from orbit to jump-start a new Terran culture, though it would be a culture far removed from anything Earth had spawned on its own. Forty percent of the population was composed of alien species, for one thing, and they would have contributions of their own. But at least humanity's home world would not be so forlorn, dusty, sad, and half-forgotten.

There was a chime from her sleeve display, and Sula looked to discover a call from Jack Danitz. She hadn't heard from him since her return to the dockyard, when she'd transmitted to him the tactics by which she'd survived Second Magaria.

Because she was in a good mood, she answered. Even Danitz's booming voice and aggressive presence failed to spoil her mood.

"I've won Second Magaria three times now!" he proclaimed. "Twice as the loyalists, and once as the Naxids. It's brilliant!"

"I trust you're giving your tactics proper credit," Sula said.

"I will, eventually," Danitz said. "But there are some egos I need to crush first."

"Well," she said, "good luck with that."

Danitz preened on the little sleeve display. "Luck

won't have anything to do with it."

By now, Sula had ceased to be amused. "Is there a reason you called me, Mr. Danitz?"

"Oh. Yes." He smiled. "I see that your impersonator got away. Would you like me to help find her?"

"The police are already looking. And she won't be masquerading as me any longer and won't be making public appearances, so I don't know where you'd start."

Danitz flashed a confident smile. "I have a few ideas."

Sula thought for a moment about whether she wanted Spendlove found, then decided she didn't care one way or another. "Go ahead, if you want. You're not about to start some kind of detective re-creationist club, are you?"

Danitz laughed. "You know, that's not a bad idea. Maybe I will."

"Good hunting, then, Mister Danitz."

"Thanks! Say, I wonder—"

Sula terminated the conversation. She pictured Danitz—tall as a signpost, spindly, bearded, in his suede boots—skulking around the alleys of Constantinople, pretending to be a detective, and the thought cheered her.

She turned to the window and looked out at the ring and the stars beyond. Somewhere out there was the wormhole gate that would lead to a new, green, uninhabited world, soon to have a city named Ermina. Perhaps it would be a place for Sula to retire, decades from now, when she decided to leave the Fleet and become someone else.

Who was she now? she wondered. After the visit to Terra, the intrigues, impersonations, threats, and murder?

Sula was the same person she'd been before. A weapon, directed not against the rebels as before but against a new clutch of enemies. Just as determined, just as isolated, living a life just as precarious as she had during the rebellion.

Everything dies. Nothing matters. Words to live by.

She looked at her faint reflection in the window, raised a hand, pointed it like a pistol.

That's what this is about, she thought.

"Bang," she said, and lowered her hand.

This is who I am, she thought.

About the Author

WALTER JON WILLIAMS has written more than thirty volumes of fiction, in addition to works in film, television, comics, and the gaming field. A Nebula Award–winning author, he's appeared on the bestseller lists of the *Times* (U.K.) and the *New York Times,* and is a world traveler, scuba diver, and a black belt in Kenpo Karate.

He began his career by writing historical fiction, the sea adventure series Privateers & Gentlemen, before moving into a new career as a science fiction writer. The first novel to attract serious public attention was *Hardwired.*

He's written cyberpunk (*Hardwired, Voice of the Whirlwind, Angel Station*), near-future thrillers (*This Is Not a Game, The Rift*), classic space opera (*Dread Empire's Fall*), "new" space opera (*Aristoi*), post-cyberpunk epic fantasy new weird (*Metropolitan* and *City on Fire*), and of course the world's only gothic western science fiction police procedural (*Days of Atonement*).

He's also a prolific writer of short fiction, including contributions to George R. R. Martin's Wild Cards project.

He's also maintained a foot in the gaming industry, having written RPGs based on Privateers & Gentlemen and *Hardwired,* contributed to the alternate-reality game *Last Call Poker,* and written the dialog for the Electronic Arts game *Spore.*

TOR·COM

Science fiction. Fantasy. The universe.

And related subjects.

*

More than just a publisher's website, *Tor.com*
is a venue for **original fiction, comics,** and
discussion of the entire field of SF and fantasy,
in all media and from all sources. Visit our site
today—and join the conversation yourself.